Dan was completely taken aback. "What? Why did I call you Princess? I don't know. You just seem—"

She boldly met his eyes. "Don't *ever* call me that."

"Why?"

"I—I don't remember. But I *don't* like it."

"Fine. But I've got to call you something." Dan refused to delve into the princess thing. Tomorrow hopefully, he wouldn't be calling her anything at all. "How about Angel?"

A slow, soft smile broke over her face. "You think I'm an angel, Dan?"

That smile gripped him and he lost himself, lost his mind and his control for a moment. "I think you've got the face of an angel. I'm not sure about the rest of you—" his traitorous gaze traveled the length of her "—yet."

Dear Reader,

Let Silhouette Desire rejuvenate your romantic spirit in May with six new passionate, powerful and provocative love stories.

Our compelling yearlong twelve-book series DYNASTIES: THE BARONES continues with *Where There's Smoke...* (#1507) by Barbara McCauley, in which a fireman as courageous as he is gorgeous saves the life and wins the heart of a Barone heiress. Next, a domineering cowboy clashes with a mysterious woman hiding on his ranch, in *The Gentrys: Cinco* (#1508), the launch title of THE GENTRYS, a new three-book miniseries by Linda Conrad.

A night of passion brings new love to a rancher who lost his family and his leg in a tragic accident in *Cherokee Baby* (#1509) by reader favorite Sheri WhiteFeather. *Sleeping with Beauty* (#1510) by Laura Wright features a sheltered princess who slips past the defenses of a love-shy U.S. Marshal. A dynamic Texan inspires a sperm-bank-bound thirtysomething stranger to try conceiving the old-fashioned way in *The Cowboy's Baby Bargain* (#1511) by Emilie Rose, the latest title in Desire's BABY BANK theme promotion. And in *Her Convenient Millionaire* (#1512) by Gail Dayton, a pretend marriage between a Palm Beach socialite and her millionaire beau turns into real passion.

Why miss even one of these brand-new, red-hot love stories? Get all six and share in the excitement from Silhouette Desire this month.

Enjoy!

Melissa Jeglinski
Senior Editor, Silhouette Desire

Please address questions and book requests to:
Silhouette Reader Service
U.S.: 3010 Walden Ave., P.O. Box 1325, Buffalo, NY 14269
Canadian: P.O. Box 609, Fort Erie, Ont. L2A 5X3

Sleeping with Beauty
LAURA WRIGHT

Silhouette® Desire®

Published by Silhouette Books

America's Publisher of Contemporary Romance

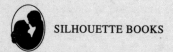

SILHOUETTE BOOKS

RECYCLED PAPER
RECYCLED PAPER

ISBN 0-373-76510-X

SLEEPING WITH BEAUTY

Copyright © 2003 by Laura Wright

Visit Silhouette at www.eHarlequin.com

Printed in U.S.A.

LAURA WRIGHT

has spent most of her life immersed in the world of acting, singing and competitive ballroom dancing. But when she started writing romance, she knew she'd found the true desire of her heart! Although born and raised in Minneapolis, Laura has also lived in New York City, Milwaukee and Columbus, Ohio. Currently, she is happy to have set down her bags and made Los Angeles her home. And a blissful home it is—one that she shares with her theatrical production manager husband, Daniel, and three spoiled dogs. During those few hours of downtime from her beloved writing, Laura enjoys going to art galleries and movies, cooking for her hubby, walking in the woods, lazing around lakes, puttering in the kitchen and frolicking with her animals. Laura would love to hear from you. You can write to her at P.O. Box 5811 Sherman Oaks, CA 91413 or e-mail her at laurawright@laurawright.com.

To my Dan…

Prologue

Princess Catherine Olivia Ann Thorne sat pole straight between her father and her aunt Fara at the head table, watching the people of Llandaron eat, drink, dance and be merry. Tonight, missing only the eldest brother, Alex, they celebrated the return of her younger brother Maxim and his wife, Fran, from their month-long honeymoon. The family celebrated the couple's fantastic news of their pregnancy.

And they celebrated love.

Music drifted up from the twelve-piece orchestra, encircling the brightly lit room. Scents of roast lamb and summer heather joined in the dreamy rotation, creating a blithe, warm atmosphere in the ballroom.

But inside Cathy a cold heaviness dwelled.

Her gaze moved over her brother and new sister-in-law as they danced, so close, eyes locked, mouths turned up into intimate smiles.

Anyone could see how desperately in love they were. And it wasn't that Cathy begrudged them such happiness. Not in the least. She loved her brother with all her heart, and thought the world of Fran. She just wanted to feel a little of that happiness—a little of that love—for herself.

"Your tour of Eastern Europe has been extended another month, Catherine."

Cathy's stomach clenched at her father's words. She'd only returned from Australia three days ago, yet her social secretary had her scheduled to leave for Russia at the beginning of next week.

And now, another month was being tacked on.

"You look pale, Cathy dear," Fara remarked, the beautiful old woman's violet eyes narrowed with concern.

The big, white-haired bear of a man touched his daughter's gloved hand. "Are you feeling all right?"

"Yes, Father." *Actually, no, Father.* The mask of composed princess fought the restive, reckless woman who resided deep in Cathy's heart. Over the last several months something inside her, in her mind and soul and blood, had started to wilt. Frustration built day by day, tour after tour. Granted, she loved the visits, and especially her charity work, but she was exhausted.

Cathy stood up, dropped her silk napkin beside her untouched plate. "I'm very tired. If you'll excuse me, Father, Fara."

She barely waited for them to nod. With a grace

she was born and bred to, she glided out of the room, into the empty hall and up the stairs, her lavender ball gown swishing against her unsteady legs. Months of supervised, heavily guarded travels, dictated protocol, and hounding press made her need for privacy akin to her need for air. The quiet, albeit temporary, sanctuary of her bedroom sounded like heaven.

But the way to her room was blocked.

"That mane of amber curls and those wide amethyst eyes."

Perched on the landing stood a portly woman, gnarled with age and garbed in a long tank dress of red and purple, ropes of tangerine beads hanging from her neck. Cathy didn't recognize her.

"You are every bit as beautiful as I told your mother you'd be, lass."

Cathy gripped the banister. "You knew my mother?"

"Aye. I knew the late queen." The woman's thin lips twisted into a cynical smile. "When you were just a speck in your mother's belly, I asked Her Royal Highness to allow me to read your future. But she refused my gift. Laughed at me, she did."

The woman's anger sat like a spoiled child between them, immobile unless appeased. A strange surge of unease coursed through Cathy. "Who are you?"

The old woman ignored the query. "I gave the king and queen my gift regardless. Aye, I told them that you would be beautiful and kind and clever. I told them that you would be spirited and brave." Her large brown eyes darkened. "I told them that if they did not take great care of you…"

Cold fingers inched up Cathy's spine as the woman's voice trailed off. But she refused to show her fear. She forced on her finest royal countenance and said, "I think you should finish the story."

The old woman's yellow smile widened. "I told your father and mother that if they did not take great care, they would lose ye."

"Lose me?" she exclaimed.

"Aye."

Deportment all but dropped away. "What are you talking about?"

"Cathy, you up there?"

The call shot between Cathy and the woman, breaking the trance that seemed to hold them both captive. Whirling around, her heart pounding in her chest, Cathy saw Fran coming up the steps, her blond hair bouncing about her shoulders.

"What's wrong, Cath?" Her sister-in-law's deep brown eyes were filled with apprehension.

"This woman. She's—"

Fran cocked her head, glanced past her. "What woman?"

Cathy stilled, her pulse pounding a feverish rhythm in her blood. Slowly, she turned. The woman was gone.

On legs that had gone from unsteady to leaden, Cathy lumbered up the stairs, saying nothing, Fran following closely behind her. Cathy tried not to wonder where the old woman had disappeared to, or if there had been a woman at all. She tried not to think that perhaps she'd gone crazy.

As they entered the bedroom, Fran asked softly, "Are you all right, Cath?"

Cathy sat on her bed, shoulders falling forward. No, she wasn't all right. She was completely and totally overwhelmed. She turned to Fran and explained, "I'm a twenty-five-year-old woman who's rarely been alone, rarely known happiness and never known love. I'm so bloody tired of living on other people's terms." She searched her new sister's eyes. "Do you understand what that's like, Fran?"

Fran sat down beside her, took her hand. "Yes, actually I do. Until I met your brother, I hadn't lived at all."

"Why is that, do you think? Were you afraid to live or—"

"I think I was afraid to believe that love existed for me." A soft smile graced Fran's mouth, the smile of a woman who now knew differently. "I'd been hurt pretty badly, and I didn't want to feel that kind of pain again. But your brother offered me a second chance."

Cathy sighed. "I'd like a *first chance*—to live. I think I deserve one."

"Of course you do."

Seven years of thoughts, plans, midnight fantasies and heartfelt hopes danced through Cathy's brain. Was she brave enough? Weary enough? Desperate enough to grab hold, to take what she wanted?

Perhaps the old woman had come with a warning, not just a story from the past. A warning from her mother and maybe even from Cathy herself, that if she continued on this path, living in unhappiness, not really living at all, she'd truly be lost.

A shadow of apprehension grazed her heart, but she brushed it away. "You're my sister now, Fran. Can I count on you?"

Fran squeezed her hand. "Just tell me what I can do."

"Help me pack."

One

Mosquitoes nibbled on her neck, unseen animals made sounds she didn't recognize and the package of oatmeal she'd consumed an hour ago sat like a steel plate in her stomach.

But Cathy had never felt happier in her life.

Three days ago, dressed in typical college-backpacking-across-Europe grungewear, armed with a fake passport she'd paid dearly for and an American accent she'd learned to flawlessly imitate during her many years of travel, Cathy had followed through on her seven-year-old plan and left Llandaron for her own tour of the United States.

True to her word, Fran had helped Cathy pack and get to the airport. And as the burden of giving the king his daughter's runaway note was a great one,

Cathy thought it best not to tell her sister-in-law where she was headed.

During the entire flight to New York, Cathy had worried about her father's reaction. But once she'd arrived in the Big Apple, she'd forced herself to let go of her concerns. Regardless of his anxiety over her whereabouts he would have to understand that in her current state of mind, she was of no use to him or to the people he wanted her to visit.

From New York, she'd taken another flight to Dallas, then another to Denver, then a cab to the hiking company's office, enjoying her freedom every step of the way.

Her plans for the trip had gone off without a hitch, and she was certain that no one had followed her.

She grinned. She was fairly certain of it anyway.

To her right, the morning sun filtered through a stand of fragrant pine, as though eager to spotlight the needled path she walked. To her left, shards of silvery-white water cascaded down a canyon to a rushing river. The gentle slap of water against rock lulled her, yet drove her farther, up into the majestic mountains. The Colorado Rockies were just as beautiful as her old friend from finishing school had told her they would be.

A perfect place for a weary princess to escape.

As requested, the hiking company had dropped Cathy off at the base of the mountains, where the trails began, climbed and spread. Armed with a full backpack of supplies, a walking stick, pepper spray and an emergency beeper, she hiked deep into the mountains. Each night she followed the map to one of the hiking company's sparse little cabins. She ate what was packed for her, slept on the hard, thin mattress that was provided and never complained.

She embraced her freedom, the adventure and the survival.

The word *survival* nicked her on the ear, made her pause midstep on the precarious stretch of narrow trail. Instinct gripped her sharply. She cocked her head to one side, listened.

She'd heard something.

Ten feet below, water smacked against rock. High above, birds twittered gaily in the swaying trees. She'd heard it all before.

Yet, there was something else.

Before she could examine the sound further, all thought suddenly froze in her brain. Barreling out of the woods came a horse and rider. Black stallion and shadowed man, heading straight for her. Time seemed to slow as river and hooves pounded.

Cathy's heartbeat hammered in her chest, stumbling as she tried to think. She could only stare, motionless, as the snorting stallion drew nearer, nearer, then reared.

Cathy scrambled to get out of its way. Left, then right. Dust and pine needles flew and crackled. But in her haste, her foot caught on a rock still wet with dew.

Down she went, her backpack slipping off her shoulders, tumbling away, over the ravine. A scream escaped her throat as she saw only rock—her last thought on the old woman's prediction.

"I told them they would lose ye…"

Then the ground rose up to claim her.

* * *

A violent blast of curses echoed through the mountain air. Gut tight, Dan Mason jumped off his now-lame horse and scrambled over to the woman. He touched her hand, but she didn't move, didn't make a sound. Where the hell had she come from anyway? he wondered, gaze flickering up and around. These paths were always clear. Especially at 6:00 a.m., when a man was looking to run from the demons of the night before, month before—years before.

As gently as a man used to dealing with hard-core criminals could manage, he rolled the woman to her back, brushed aside strands of long tawny curls and touched the base of her throat. A strong, steady pulse beat against his fingers. He leaned close, felt her easy breath against his jaw.

He shook his head, released a weighty sigh.

With the eyes of a deputy U.S. marshal, he assessed her condition. She didn't appear to have any broken bones. She did, however, have a ruthless bruise on her forehead, a bruise that, thankfully, swelled outward.

As his gaze moved over her heart-shaped face, those marshal eyes turned into the eyes of a man. He couldn't help it. He was base, a needful bastard. And she looked like an angel. Cupid-bow lips, satin skin, long neck. Then there was that firm chin that hinted at a real stubborn streak.

His gaze flickered downward. Thin gray sweatshirt, worn jeans and man-killer curves.

He inhaled sharply, called himself a depraved idiot

and forced his game face back on. All in all, she was a typical hiker with typical hiking gear. Except for the boots. No mistaking. Those were top of the line. The woman had money.

The river roared from its bed ten feet down, snatching his attention like a fire alarm, spitting up spray. A muscle jumped in Dan's jaw. She could've gone over the edge.

He leaned toward her, whispered sharply, "Lady, wake up."

He got nothing. Nothing but one helluva sweet scent.

"Lady, can you hear me?"

A soft moan slipped from those pale-pink lips. She moved slightly, her face twisting, no doubt in pain. Pain was good, he thought. But getting her to wake up was better.

In a tone more suited to press criminals than soothe victims, he urged her on, "You've got to wake up now. Open your eyes and look at me."

At that, tawny lashes fluttered, then opened. Eyes the color of violets stared up at him, made his chest constrict.

"Can you hear me?"

Blinking drunkenly, she nodded.

"You out here alone?"

Confusion swept her angel face as she uttered hoarsely, "I don't know."

"Do you feel dizzy? Sick to your stomach?"

"A little."

He frowned. He knew something about head

wounds. And this sounded like a concussion. "Your head hurt?"

"Aches." Her responses came out as uneasy whispers. But it was the look in her eyes, the confusion, the fear that had his teeth clenching in undisguised anger.

He could see another woman, his partner, his fiancée, face pale, lips parted, staring up at a six-foot-five heavily muscled fugitive who was supposed to be on the other side of her gun.

Had Janice looked like this woman? Frightened, desperate?

Dan's jaw threatened to crack. That horrific night had happened over four years ago, for chrissakes. How many times was he going to go through it, relive it? He hadn't been there for her, case closed—couldn't've been there for her. He'd been tied to that hospital bed, a bullet lodged in his thigh.

And hell, the bastard was behind bars where he belonged now anyway. Granted, a little more bruised and beaten than when he'd last faced a cell. Something Dan had seen to, something that had gotten his ass suspended and sent up to a mountain cabin to think about what he'd done, and if all went according to plan, feel remorse for it.

He grunted. His superiors were going to be waiting a long time for that to happen.

On a pained sigh, the woman in front of him let her lids close. All questions, all memories dropped to the back of his mind for more pressing and present matters.

This woman needed a doctor. But how was he going to contact one? Her pack had fallen over the crag, had to be a mile downstream by now. He didn't have a cell phone.

Truth was, he hadn't wanted any contact with the outside world. And now this woman was forcing his hand.

Options were few. Town was a full day's ride away.

With a sharp sigh, he gathered her small frame into his arms, snatched Rancon's reins and headed back to his cabin.

Two
―――

Thumbnail sketches of flowered hillsides and rocky coastlines and one dangerously handsome man with dark, probing eyes drifted in and out of her muddled brain, warring with the sting over her left eyebrow and the dull pounding in her skull.

From far off she heard a moan. A feminine sound, but low and gravel-like. She wanted to run toward the woman, embrace her, whisper soothing words. But where was she?

"You need to wake up."

The male voice slashed through the fog of her mind. The sting turned sharp as she strained to do as she was commanded. She tried to move, tried to shake her head. But her limbs felt heavy, water-filled. All she wanted to do was sleep, just sleep.

"I know you hear me," came the masculine growl

once again. "Open your eyes or there's going to be trouble."

She felt fingers, strong and cool at the base of her throat. She inhaled sharply at the touch, taking in the scents of pine and leather and sweat and...male...

With great effort, she forced her eyes open. Inches from her was a man—a ruthlessly handsome man with mussed black hair, piercing eyes, obstinate jaw and previously broken nose that she'd seen...

When?

Muscles tense with fear, she stared into those brown eyes of his, dark as chocolate, melted, *hot* chocolate, and uttered a hoarse "Who are you?"

The man's hard gaze moved boldly over her face, hovered near her mouth, then lifted to her eyes and narrowed. "You first."

Confused, she felt her forehead crease, but she didn't argue with him. For, a more alarming predicament was rising up, biting her on the ear. When she opened her mouth, fully expecting her name to slip out easily, thoughtlessly...nothing emerged.

Terror twisted in her belly, shooting off balls of anxiety that had no direction, no catcher. She began to shake. Her throat went dry as a summer wind. She shut her eyes, willed herself to concentrate, to relax. This was ridiculous. The truth was there, on the tip of her tongue, who she was and where she'd come from.

Moments passed.

Nothing came.

She lifted her eyelids. "I don't know who I am."

A curse, ripe and hot, fell from his lips.

There had to be a logical explanation for this whole situation, she reasoned, must be. She just had to think, take a moment and concentrate.

Forcing a calm tone she hardly felt, she asked, "Are we lovers? Married?"

He snorted. "No."

"Friends, then? Acquaintances—"

"No."

Nervously, she looked around the room. She was in a small bedroom, sparsely furnished with just the bed, an old dresser and rocking chair. Above, the ceiling sported scores of rustic wood logs, while the large windows in front of her peered out over imposing mountains.

A log cabin.

And none of it rang one tiny bell of recognition.

"This is your house?"

He offered only a curt nod.

She shifted nervously under the covers. "This is your bed?"

"Yes." An almost imperceptible glimmer of danger passed through his eyes. "I only have the one. Thought you'd be more comfortable here than on the couch."

"I…appreciate that."

With another quick nod, he stood. "You should probably get some rest."

Without thought, she reached out, grabbed his wrist. "Wait. Please."

He glanced down, frowned. "What is it?"

"I'm sorry." Blushing, she released her grip on him. "I just want to know what happened—"

"Later. Rest now." He turned, started for the door.

"Can you at least tell me your name?" she asked.

He stopped but didn't turn around. "Dan."

"Dan what?"

"That's all you need to know."

And with that, he left the room. Left a woman with no memory and a million questions staring after him.

As twilight arrested and called in the day, Dan hauled in the wood he'd chopped that morning and dropped it beside the fireplace.

Physical labor of any kind was his saving grace. If his mind dropped back to the past or shot into the future, he'd just grab the ax and have at it. Sometimes mucking out Rancon's stall emptied his mind as well.

But not tonight.

The mystery woman with her violet eyes, I-need-you voice and fancy accent was sleeping in his bed, between his sheets—had been for the past four hours—and the thought was slowly but surely making him nuts.

He was now entirely over the fact that she could be a criminal or a spy or some such bull. Now his suspicious nature had turned into something far more dangerous: desire. With just a glance, that woman had his blood pumping and his curiosity piqued—two things he hadn't felt in a very long time.

Two things he'd never wanted to feel again.

Bottom line, if he wanted to stay marginally sane, she had to go. And soon. He wasn't looking for romance. Anything close to that had rendered itself defunct four years ago.

Besides, foreign debutantes weren't his thing. Especially foreign debutantes with zero memory. No doubt she had family, friends and some top-drawer kinda guy from England or Scotland—or wherever she was from—waiting for a word of her whereabouts.

After lighting a fire in the fireplace, Dan grabbed a beer from the fridge, cracked it open, took a healthy swallow, then plunked his body down on the couch. Tomorrow, if the woman was up for it, he'd take her into town, drop her off at the doctor's and head back, back to silence and solitude and the always interesting notion of peace.

Dan paused, beer halfway to his mouth. "You shouldn't be out of bed."

He heard a small gasp behind him, glanced over his shoulder. Hands behind her back, the petite beauty stood a few feet away in her rumpled hiking gear with the moonlight beaming through the window, illuminating her face. She looked a little dazed. But beautiful. Too beautiful.

He turned back around. "You need to rest."

"I know." She walked around the couch, sat down beside him, crossed her legs at the ankles. "I woke up and felt a little scared, so I thought…"

"You thought you'd come hang out with me?"

"If you don't mind."

Mind? Why should he mind? Just because his body revved to life whenever he looked at her? "No, I don't mind. But don't make the mistake of thinking that it's any safer out here."

He watched her lips part, shock brighten those

killer eyes, and pink color those high cheekbones. He tilted his beer toward her, trying for a lighter mood. "Thirsty?"

Her smile was short and tentative. "No, thanks."

"No, probably not good for you." Neither the beer nor the company.

"Not tonight anyway. Maybe another time."

Her words snaked through him. Innocent enough, but they were sulfur to a match that had been stripped for a long time.

His hand tightened on the neck of the beer bottle as he watched her brush a strand of long curly hair away from her face, hair that reflected several shades of red and blond and brown in the blaze of firelight.

Aside from the bruise on her forehead, she really did have the look of an angel about her.

The kind of look a devil like him steered clear of.

He took a pull on his beer, dropped back against the couch and asked, "Are you feeling any better?"

"A little tired. My body aches. But otherwise, not too bad."

"How about your head? That fall you took was pretty serious."

She inhaled sharply. "I fell? Where? In the mountains? Why?"

"Take it easy, lady. Look, all I know is that you and my horse scared the bejesus out of each other this morning, that you both ended up injured and that as soon as it's possible, we'll get you back to who and where you belong." He took another swallow of beer. "Now, are you going to tell me how that head of yours is doing?"

"All right," she said, a soft smile twitching her lips. "The pain's gone and the head's still attached."

"And the memory?"

That smile wavered. "I still don't remember anything."

"You will."

"Well, if you say so, then I'll believe it."

It was as though someone had wrapped a tire iron around the stone he used for a heart and squeezed. "Why is that?"

"I don't know, I just...I feel like I can trust you."

He shot her a cynical twist of a smile. "You shouldn't trust anyone."

Confusion lit her eyes. And right then Dan knew exactly where she'd come from: Innocent Avenue, round the corner from Sheltered Street, in the never-polluted city of Naive. Those kind of people made him crazy. You had to see the world for what it was if you wanted to survive. Didn't she know that?

Of course she didn't.

"You hungry?" he asked, hoping to redirect both their attentions.

She nodded eagerly. "But I'd like to wash up first if you don't mind."

"I don't mind at all. How about a shower?"

Her eyes went wide. "A shower?"

Dan wanted to laugh. Really he did, that is, if he could remember how. "That was just a gentlemanly offer, not a come-on."

"A come-on?"

"A line. A play to get you naked, wet and soapy."

Her pretty face glowed with pink embarrassment. "Oh."

This was getting out of control. This prim-and-proper thing she had going was really getting under his skin, making his body ache like hell. On an irritated grumble, Dan seized her hand, helped her to her feet and led her into the bedroom and over to his closet. After grabbing a few extra-large items that wouldn't tempt him, he handed them to her. "Here."

"What are these?"

"Clean clothes."

"I know that," she said. "I was just wondering if these were *your* clothes?"

"Yeah. Gotta problem with that?"

For a moment she just stared at him, then shook her head and said, "Not in the least."

"Good." He led her to the bathroom door, beckoned for her to walk past him. And as soon as she did, he followed.

It took her about three seconds to notice him. And when she did, when she turned to look at him, that stubborn chin of hers was tilted up. "Where do you think you're going, Dan?"

He pointed past her. "In there."

She blinked. "With me?"

"That's right."

"Absolutely not!"

"Listen, lady, as I said before, this isn't a come-on."

She crossed her arms over her chest. "Then what is it exactly?"

He growled irritably and stalked past her, jerked

open the navy-blue shower curtain and turned on the hot water. "You have a head injury. I need to be here in case something happens."

"Something like what?"

"Like you could get dizzy, faint, keel over—"

She shook her head. "I'm feeling much better now. Nothing like that is going to happen."

He shoved a white towel at her. "That's what I'm here to make sure of."

She didn't move, just stared at him. "Perhaps I'll take the shower another time."

Leaning against the wall, he expelled a breath and said, "Oh, for chrissakes, I'm doing you a favor here. Do you really think this is how I want to spend my night? Standing guard outside a shower curtain?"

She shrugged, gripped the towel and clothing closer to her body. Honestly, she had good reason to be suspicious. She didn't know who he was. Didn't know who *she* was.

But despite the fact that she made fire erupt inside him, he wasn't a total jerk. He wasn't about to take advantage of a naked woman with a head injury and no memory.

Unless she asked him to, of course.

"Look, Princess, the curtain is a dark color. I won't be seeing a thing, okay?"

She went stiff as a mannequin at his words, except for the faint twitch under her right eye. Teeth clenched, she fairly sputtered, "Why did you call me that?"

He was completely taken aback by this unexpected

reaction: "What? Why did I call you what? Princess? I don't know. You just seem—"

She boldly met his eyes, all Rambo and don't-mess-with-me. Damn appealing. "Don't *ever* call me that."

"Why?"

"I…I don't remember. But I *don't* like it." Even over the sound of bathwater rapping against porcelain, the gravity in her voice was evident.

"Fine. But I gotta call you something."

The bristles retracted somewhat as she seemed to think this over. "How about Beatrice?"

He frowned. "Beatrice? Where did that come from?"

She shrugged. "It's a nice enough name. And far better than the P word."

Dan refused to delve into the princess thing. Tomorrow, hopefully, he wouldn't be calling her anything at all. But for tonight, there needed to be something. And Beatrice didn't suit her. Actually, he wasn't sure what suited her. Mystery woman. Innocent one minute, full of fire the next.

"How about Angel?"

A slow, soft smile broke on her face. "You think I'm an angel?"

Her smile gripped him low in the gut. Match struck rough surface and he lost himself, lost his mind and his control for a moment. "I think you got the face of an angel. I'm not sure about the rest of you…"

His traitorous gaze traveled the length of her as his foolish mouth uttered, "Yet."

What the hell was he thinking playing this game

with her? Dan admonished himself seconds later. A game that would be over before it even had a chance to begin.

That was an easy one. He *wasn't* thinking.

He watched her lips part, hoped she was going to scold him with that sweet brogue of hers, tell him to get out and go straight to hell.

But she didn't. She licked her lower lip, slow and seductive and totally unguarded.

He snatched open the shower curtain. Hot steam poured into the tiny bathroom. "Let's go. Clothes off, Angel. Time to get wet."

Three

Hot water pelted her aching muscles. She closed her eyes and tilted her head back, allowing the water to cleanse her wound and her spirit. The fresh citrus scent of shampoo drifted from her hair, while the soapy suds slid down her back, over her buttocks, thighs and calves.

All anxiety slipped down the drain with the bubbles and the day's dirt.

''How's it going in there?''

Her pulse kicked and her skin tightened at the gruff query.

So much for relaxation.

Dan stood guard outside the sway of a shower curtain, the outline of his exceptional frame a mere inches from her naked body—strangely, a body and a face she'd hardly recognized when she'd spied herself in the mirror earlier. The strangeness of this entire situation was staggering, from the blank canvas that was her mind to the thrilling shots of awareness she felt whenever her rescuer was near.

But there was nothing for it. She was going to stay here tonight, in his cabin in the woods, feel an overwhelming surge of need and try like hell to keep her wits about her.

Actually, step one of that strategy had gone off without a hitch. Before she'd removed her clothing and stepped under the spray, she'd removed Dan. When she was safely behind the blue curtain, she'd told him he could return, as per their agreement.

And they'd had to make an agreement. The man was incredibly stubborn and protective and arrogant and handsome and—

"Angel?" The pet name glided over her heated skin like the soft, cotton washcloth in her hand.

"Yes?"

"I asked how it's going in there."

"Everything's fine. Just fine. Thank you. No worries. Or problems." Except for the fact that she was rambling on like an idiot.

"You sure you don't need any help?"

"Positive. Except…"

"Except for what?"

"Well, there is one thing—soap."

"You don't like it?"

"There is none."

"Oh. Sorry about that. I must've used up the last of it this morning."

"Perhaps I could use the shampoo as a—"

"No, no, I'll get you another bar."

Over the thrashing water, she heard a cabinet door open, then the sound of paper being torn. And before she could even think, blink or gasp, a hand—Dan's hand—shot through one side of the curtain.

"Here you go."

She mumbled a quick, "Thank you," but didn't take the soap from his hand. In fact, she didn't move at all.

She felt incredibly exposed as she stared at his hand, at his long, tapered fingers wrapped around that pale-blue cake of soap. Shudders of electricity began in her stomach, then dropped lower as her mind conjured images of that hand cupping something else...cupping her, her face, her hip, her breast.

"It's the manly scented stuff, but it gets the job done."

Clearing her throat, she managed to say, "I'm sure that it does."

All she had to do was take the bloody bar. What was wrong with her? When she'd fallen and hit her head, had she unleashed some lusty side of her that had gone unchecked? Because, Lord, she felt as though she'd never had thoughts like this.

"Aren't you going to take it, Angel?"

With an unsteady hand, she reached out. Her fingers wrapped around his, eased the bar from his hand.

Soft and wet met dry and rough.

Her breath came out in a rush. Her fingers lingered. So did his.

"Angel?"

She snatched her hand back. The soap slipped,

dropped into the tub with a thud. She stared at it, unable to go near it. "I'm almost done in here," she called out. "I just have to rinse off. You can go. Really. I can dress myself."

He was silent for a moment, then, "You sure?"

"Quite sure." Her tone excessively firm, she added, "Now, please go. I'm fine. I'll be dressed and out in a few moments."

"All right. But careful getting out. It's slippery."

When he left, she snatched up the notorious bar of soap and leaned against the shower wall, tried to regain her composure. Around her, the steam moved, breathed, like a living being.

Suddenly, a memory tugged at her mind. She'd been here, or in some place like this, surrounded by some kind of white haze, before. And more than once.

She tried to claim more of the impression, but the vision evaporated and she was left with only current memories, ones that made her skin tighten with a frightening sense of excitement she didn't recognize but was tempted to explore.

She stood directly under the shower's spray, hoping to rid herself of such thoughts and feelings. But as soon as she touched the fragrant bar of soap to her skin, she was lost.

For, just moments ago, it had been in his hand.

Nothing fancy. But it'll do.

Dan scooped up some of the warmed, canned spaghetti into two bowls, placed a few slices of buttered bread on a plate and brought it all to the table. He was no cook. Too much career, too little time for anything else.

"May I help?"

Dan turned at the silky-sounding offer, watched the woman walk out of the bathroom, rosy-cheeked, hair down and damp. "Nope. It's all set."

She was wearing his clothes. Big and baggy clothes. But that didn't stop his imagination from running wild. Just as it had during her shower.

He'd stood there, back to the curtain, trying to stop himself from thinking, from breaking the zipper on his jeans, and from sliding open the curtain and joining her. And now, here she stood, dressed in his gray sweats. Her skin, her thighs, the backs of her knees, her breasts, all brushing against the fabric.

Dan forced himself to get back under control, back to the hard-nosed lawman he was. Maybe the boys down at the office were playing a trick on him. Maybe his superiors had sent this sexy creature up here to make him nuts, make him cave, make him so desperate for the world of the living that he'd admit he was wrong for messing up the perp responsible for killing his fiancée.

"Everything looks wonderful," she remarked, glancing around the table.

It sure as hell did… "Clothes fit all right?"

She lifted the sweatshirt just enough for him to see the waistband and one blessed inch of flat stomach. "These pants are a tad large. I have to hold them up with one hand, but I don't mind."

Heat pounded him in the groin. This was too much.

He stalked into the kitchen, fumbling around in a drawer, grabbed a piece of rope and came back.

"Lift the sweatshirt again."

"Why?"

"Just do it."

Tentatively, she did as he instructed. He had the rope around her waist in one second, tied in another. "There."

She stared up at him, an uncertain smile playing around her mouth. "Much better. Thank you."

He should've taken a step back, run out the friggin' front door, but he didn't. He stood there, looked down into her eyes and wanted to haul her against him, cover her mouth with his, feel her tongue…

He scrubbed a hand over his jaw.

It had been a long time since he'd stood this close to a woman and felt a pull so strong it fairly knocked him off his feet.

Getting involved with someone in the past four years, even sexually, had seemed too easy and totally undeserved. No matter how masochistic it sounded, he felt the need to punish himself, deny himself, always and forever. After a while, he'd just forgotten to want.

Then, this violet-eyed temptress had stepped into his path, got herself hurt, got herself dropped between his sheets. Thank God she was only going to be around here for one night.

He held out a chair for her. "Have a seat."

She sat with her back to the fire, her wet hair glowing tricolor fire. "If I didn't say this before, I really appreciate all that you've done. I'm sure I've inconvacationed you terribly, and as soon as you deem me well enough to travel, I'll be out of your way."

"It's not a problem." *What a bold-faced lie.*

"But it *is* a bother. Were you on holiday? Is this your vacation spot?"

"No."

"Oh. Do you live up here year-round then?"

"No."

"Then what are you doing up here?"

His gaze lifted. He watched as she twirled her spaghetti against a spoon. "You know, you ask a lot of questions for someone with no memory."

Spaghetti stopped twirling, forehead creased. "Are you in some type of law enforcement, Dan?"

His eyes narrowed. "Why would you ask that?"

"You're very suspicious of me. I doubt very much that I am a criminal."

He doubted it, too, but after five years as a cop and ten as a marshal, you wondered about everyone. Especially someone you were attracted to. Could make for big problems.

"Perhaps I'm asking questions," she began, returning to her dinner, "because I'm frustrated. I have no memory, no identification, no personal effects. Perhaps I'm asking questions because I think learning about someone else's past might trigger memories of my own."

"Is that really what you think?"

"Yes."

The pasta suddenly felt like worms in Dan's mouth. He dropped his fork onto his plate, sat back in his chair. "I have no past."

She raised her gaze, studied him. "What does that mean?"

"That means, Angel, that I don't want to talk about it." He ground out the words, frustration building inside him.

"Sounds rather daunting. Maybe you would feel better if you did."

"I don't think so."

"Let's try and—"

"You know what I feel?" he interrupted.

"What?"

"Tired." He pushed away from the table, took his bowl into the kitchen, dropped it in the sink, enjoying the crashing sound it made.

Sure, he owed this woman his care, his protection. But his personal life was none of her business. It was no one's business. "You can take my bed tonight. I'll sleep on the couch."

"The couch is very small. I'd hate to have you be so uncomfortable."

A swift jolt of desire rose up and bit him on the butt. She was making him crazy with all her questions and good manners. He spun around. "We could share the bed."

Her gaze met his for a moment, then dropped to her plate. "No, no." Her cheeks flushed pink. "I didn't mean... The offer for your bed is a very generous one."

He exhaled. "Tomorrow, we'll head into town. See the doctor."

"All right," she agreed, taking a dainty bite of pasta.

And the doctor could take her off his hands for good. Then things would get back to normal. Fishing and cussing and forgetting about the past. He could go back to eating in peace and not thinking about beautiful violet-eyed women and where his soap had been.

At that moment, the beautiful violet-eyed woman in question stood up and began collecting plates and bowls. "You know, you're a very good cook, Dan. Was there fresh thyme in the tomato sauce?"

The woman had to be a diplomat or something. He shrugged. "You'd have to ask Chef Boyardee."

"You have a chef?"

Dan paused, rewound. Then a chuckle—an honest to goodness chuckle—escaped his dusty lungs. Leaning back against the sink, he shook his head. "Man, you really have lost your memory. The pasta's from a can."

"And so is the chef?"

He nodded.

Her face broke out into a wide grin.

His, too.

He reached for her plates and placed them in the sink, this time with only a mild clatter. She disarmed him with that smile and easy way of hers. Extraordinary.

Yet worrisome. If she could make him smile a dozen times—and laugh—all in one day, she was a bigger batch of trouble than he'd even imagined.

"You should probably head in to bed," he suggested. "I have an injured horse who needs tending."

She nodded. "Are you sure I can't help?"

"I'm sure."

"Well, thanks again for dinner."

"No problem."

"And I really hope my memory returns in the morning."

"So do I." Truer words were never spoken. "Make sure to keep the door open a crack."

"Okay. Good night." After one of those irresistible smiles, she turned and left the room.

"Good night, Angel."

Dan grabbed a beer from the fridge and went to the couch, his bed for the night. In the fireplace, the flames crackled and sputtered, fighting to stay alive. He knew their fierceness, their hunger.

For four years, he'd been crawling around on his belly, unwilling to stand up. He'd never thought he'd have the pluck.

From the bedroom, he heard the woman pull back the comforter, heard the bed dip with the weight of her body.

Around her, he had the pluck. Around her, he had the urge to stand.

He drained his beer, then headed for the front door.

Around her, he had a new hunger, dangerous and demanding.

Four

Eyes closed, body relaxed, she floated in a shallow sea of warm light, soft sand. No cares, no worries, just peace.

Dropping down beside her, he grinned, then took her hand and kissed the palm. He had that look in his eye, the one that made her weak and wanting. Waves curved, lapped against them both, between them. The man slipped a plum under her nose, then a silver plate of biscuits, still warm.

She inhaled deeply, smiled. "Tea and fruit…and biscuits."

"I don't make tea, Angel."

A gasp shot forth from deep in her throat as she forced her eyes open, forced her dreams back where they belonged. The first thing she saw was morning sunlight, yellow and brilliant.

Then she saw him.

Freshly showered and looking far more handsome than any man had a right to in jeans and a black T-shirt, Dan towered above her, a touch of amusement glinting in those deep-brown orbs of his.

Her mind reeled. Yesterday was all that she recalled; the accident, memory gone, shower, hands touching, dinner, sleep—sleep in this man's bed, the scent of him in the sheets that tangled between her legs. Her skin warmed at the thought.

"I don't make biscuits either," he said.

"What was I saying?" she asked, rubbing the sleep from her eyes.

An eyebrow shot up. "You were giving me your breakfast order."

"I wasn't."

A devilish grin tugged at his mouth. "I'm afraid you were."

If she'd given him a breakfast order, what else had she said? How long had he been standing there? "I was obviously dreaming."

He shrugged nonchalantly. "Maybe you were remembering."

"I don't think so—"

"Maybe you were remembering that you had a maid or something."

"That's ridiculous." But his suggestion didn't feel strange or wrong. She stared up at the log ceiling with its smooth waves of wood, and willed herself to remember anything; a favorite food, her parents' names…a boyfriend.

Dan shrugged pensively. "A maid, an accent,

swanky manners. But pretty open and honest—I'm thinking you don't live in the U.S.''

"I don't know." Frustration stacked up like bricks in her mind.

"Traveling alone, though, in the mountains. Why would you do something like that?''

Though her headache was gone now, the bruise above her eyebrow was still tender. The niggling ache intermingled with the aggravation she felt. ''Do you mind if we take a break from the questions? At least until after breakfast?''

"All right. But we don't have tea or biscuits.''

She pulled the covers back and sat on the edge of the bed. ''No problem. I'll make something for myself. And for you if you haven't—''

"No, actually I haven't.''

"Perfect.''

His eyes narrowed skeptically. ''You can cook?''

She stood, gave him a proud look. ''Of course I can.'' Could she cook? She felt no answer to this, no instinctual pull toward the kitchen, and sadly no recollection of what any kitchen tools were called and used for.

Oh, well. She would know soon enough if she possessed any culinary talents.

"What do you have in the kitchen?'' she asked, stretching. ''We've already covered biscuits and tea. How about eggs, bacon—''

"Before you turn into Julia Child, tell me how you're feeling this morning.''

She touched her bruise gingerly. ''Hurts a little, but other than that I'm right as rain.''

"Right as rain, huh?"

"Yes. Don't you think I look better?"

In response, his gaze slid down the length of her. She still wore his baggy sweats, but at that moment it felt as though she wore nothing at all. Strangely, the feeling didn't fill her with apprehension. Instead, pleasure flowed in her veins, unfamiliar yet wonderful.

She asked him, "Are we going to town today?"

"I don't think so. Last night I was looking through an old first-aid manual. Said you should be relatively inactive for forty-eight hours. It's a long way on foot. Too long for you."

"I could ride," she suggested.

He shook his head. "I only have the one horse and he's injured."

"Tomorrow then?"

"Yeah, tomorrow."

Dan was a good five feet away, leaning against the wall, tall, fiercely handsome, with a history of pain and suspicion and need behind his eyes. In that moment, all she wanted to do was run to him, fall into his arms, hold him as he held her. Such a strong pull for a man she hardly knew. But it was the truth. Despite his edgy manner of speaking, she liked him, felt a kinship with him. They had both forgotten their pasts—one out of choice, one not.

The air seemed to warm between them, cracking with an alarming jolt of electricity. A muscle jumped in Dan's jaw. "I'm gonna head outside, chop some more wood. I think it'll get pretty chilly again tonight."

Obviously a fire would have to be the only thing keeping them warm tonight. "I'm going to head into the kitchen then, whip up something grand."

He pushed away from the wall and walked out of the room. "There's a fire extinguisher by the front door."

"Very funny."

No flames licked at the cabin door when Dan returned with the wood, but there sure was a lot of smoke.

Drifting out of the kitchen window was a dark cloud, accompanied by the sound of coughing. Without taking the time to put his shirt back on, Dan dropped the kindling and rushed into the cabin.

Still dressed in his sweats, the woman stood at the stove fanning smoke away from two cast-iron pans.

He was at her side in seconds. "What happened here?"

She glanced over her shoulder at him, frowned. "You're going to be pleased."

"What does that mean?"

"You were right." Shaking her head woefully, she added, "I must not know how to cook."

She turned and stared up at him with those violet orbs. She looked so pathetic he couldn't stop himself from chuckling.

"Why are you laughing?" she demanded, turning back and pointing at the pans. "Look at these eggs. Gray as the ashes in the fireplace. And look at this."

He glanced over her shoulder. Thin black strips of

burnt something gaped up at him, still smoking.
"What exactly was that?"

"Bacon."

"Seriously?"

"Of course I'm being serious!"

"Well, it doesn't look all that bad," he lied.

"Really?" She turned again to look at him, a
shadow of hope crossing her eyes.

"Really."

"Not so bad you might want to try some?"

That's what a guy got for being nice. Reminded
him of the time Josh, one of his foster brothers had
begged him to try a taco at a greasy local restaurant.
Josh had just loved the place, could eat there every
day. He'd pleaded, made offers of marbles, action fig-
ures—for two whole days. The kid could've been a
top-notch hostage negotiator. But as it was, the other
side of the law had offered Josh a better deal.

Anyway, a seven-year-old Dan had gone and been
the boy's taste tester. Dan's stomach lurched in re-
membrance. That beef taco had caused him to wor-
ship the porcelain god for three whole days.

But that had been old, maybe even contaminated
food. What Angel had here was just charred. Hell, if
he could survive seventeen hours in a truck with Rank
Ron Hunnicutt waiting on a fugitive, this'd be a walk
in the park.

He grabbed a fork, scooped up a bit of the goopy,
gray eggs and took a taste. Actually, it was a crunch.

He nearly choked on a shell, but covered pretty
quickly. Or so he thought.

"Not bad, Angel."

But she was no fool. Her eyes grew liquid and weary. "I'm sorry. Excuse me. I'm just going to get a breath of fresh air."

"Angel?"

She didn't answer him. She was out the door.

"Wait a sec."

Shoulders straight, she walked even quicker, down the deck steps and onto the dirt pathway, pine needles crunching under her feet. He caught up with her next to a massive pine.

"Stop." He made his tone cop firm.

This time she did. She turned around, tears spilling down her cheeks. "For what?"

His gut tightened as he looked at her, in pain, her cheeks flushed, hands scrunched into fists at her sides. He hadn't seen a woman crying in a while, unless it was some strung-out fugitive who needed a fix.

Even as a kid, tears were few. Back in the foster home, crying wasn't permitted. If you wanted to get away with it, you had to do it at night, silently, in your bed.

He reached out, wiped a duo of tears off her upper lip. "The eggs are no big deal, Angel."

"They are to me."

"Everyone screws up sometimes."

"Even you?"

"All the time."

Her gaze fell. "It's not just the breakfast."

He stepped closer, slipped a finger under her chin and lifted her gaze to his once again. "What is it then?"

Under the shelter of the pine, where strips of warm

sunlight blasted through the heavily scented branches like white rocket fuel, she told him. "It's my memory. I'm really scared, Dan."

"That's completely understandable."

"The world feels entirely too large right now." Her gaze implored him to understand or to comfort her or to offer her answers, or all three. "What if I never remember?"

"Come here, Angel." Better judgment aside, he pulled her against him, held her tight, breathing in the clean, sweet scent of her. He'd never been the soothing type. But the lady needed it.

She let her head fall against his chest, sighed at the easy strokes he applied to her back. He wanted to tell her not to make such sounds, wanted to warn her not to press any closer. But instead he uttered a fool's promise, "We'll find out who you are. I'm not going to let anything happen to you."

She glanced up, eyes wide. "Promise?"

Dan's chest felt as if it would burst right open. He didn't want to owe anyone anything. He didn't want to be responsible for anyone, for protecting anyone, for championing anyone.

A promise. Did she even know what she was asking?

Of course she didn't.

As she looked up at him, waiting, her lips parted, he fought the need that stabbed at him. He ached to taste her, was almost ready to tell himself that it would be in the spirit of comfort, anything. Never in his life had he wanted anything more.

He lowered his head, then stopped, his mouth

inches from hers, his need warring with his demons from the past.

If he was going to help her, protect her, physical contact was out of the question. Had to be.

Her tongue darted out, wet her lower lip.

He watched, his body tense.

Then she tilted her chin up, an invitation to paradise.

He hauled her back against him and muttered into her hair, "I promise."

Even as the barn's wall clock struck nine that night, the intimacy of the day still lingered between them. Angel could feel it, in the way Dan watched her as she worked in the stable, in the telling silence earlier at dinner, in the heat she could sense every time he was near.

Her mind reflected back to the only past it could claim. A moment under a magnificent sun-kissed pine, where Dan had held her close, his mouth just a whisper away, ready to kiss her. But hadn't.

Why hadn't he? she couldn't help but wonder. Was it her memory loss that had made him pause? Or was it something more. Was it that hurt and unquenched need she saw when she looked deep into his eyes?

"That hay goes in his feeding trough."

Angel started, almost let the pitchfork in her hand fall to the floor of Rancon's stall. "Sorry."

Dan nodded in the direction of his horse, amusement behind his eyes. "I'm not the one you should be apologizing to."

Turning to the beautiful stallion, she gave him a pleading smile. "So sorry, Rancon."

The horse whinnied and his ears perked up. Angel dropped the late-night snack within his reach.

"He forgives you," Dan said, patting the horse on the flank. "This time."

Her smile turned to laughter. "I'm so glad."

After Dan gave the horse a quick brushing, he and Angel walked back to the cabin together under a sky of diamonds. A decided chill hovered in the air, just as Dan had predicted. And while he built a fire in the homey little cabin, Angel wondered if his other prediction, his silent prediction, might come true as well.

Would the fire be the only thing keeping them warm tonight?

When she came out into the living room, Dan was setting up his bed for the night. She let him go about his business, though it wasn't all that late, and walked over, snooped at the small bookshelf that sat to the right of the fireplace. Mysteries, some children's books. Then she stopped.

On top of the bookshelf sat a rather thick tome with a strip of yellow paper marking the reader's place: *The Grapes of Wrath*.

She picked it up, turned to Dan. "What is this?"

Glancing over his shoulder, he squinted. "That would be a book."

"I know it's a book," she said on a chuckle, walking over to him. "Is it yours?"

He stopped with the sheets and pillow, took the book from her. "Could be."

Hands on hips, she asked, "Why can't I get a straight answer from you?"

"Can I say something like, 'because'?"

"No."

"How about, 'That's just the kind of guy I am'?"

"Is that the kind of guy you are?"

He didn't say anything, just turned away, muttering, "The book is mine, all right?" And went back to his sheets and pillow.

Truth was, she didn't know what kind of man he was. Of course, he'd rescued her, taken care of her, fed her. But who was he outside this cabin? Who was he in the world? And why wouldn't he share that part of himself with her?

"Dan?"

"Yes?"

"How do I know that you're a good guy and not a bad guy?"

A pause, then, "You don't."

"And neither do you, really, do you?"

He glanced over his shoulder, mouth thin, caution signals flashing in his dark eyes. "I think I put too much vinegar in that salad."

Her resolve weakened a touch under that stare, but she stood firm. "No, I think you put in just enough."

"Isn't it your bedtime, Angel?"

She strode past him, took a seat on the couch. "Not yet."

"You're sitting on my bed."

"So I am." She patted the couch beside her, hoping she wasn't being too bold. "How about you read a little?"

"Come again?"

"Read a little. Out loud."

"Hell, no."

"Please, Dan."

"No."

"I really need a distraction tonight."

Dan stared down into those liquid pools of violet and felt himself frown. A distraction. Was she kidding? He crushed the down pillow he held in his fist. If Angel really needed something like that, he could show her a few other methods of distraction.

But he wasn't giving out lessons to a woman like her, a woman with no memory, a woman who unnerved him more than the first day of police academy.

He dropped down beside her, snatched the book from her hand. Reading was a helluva lot safer way to educate her, that was sure. "If you tell anyone about this—"

She grinned. "Who am I going to tell?"

"I'm not kidding."

"All right. Cross my heart."

Like a wolf with a gazelle in sight, he watched her trace the first half of the X across her breast with her fingertip, then switch angles and trace down the slope of the opposite breast. Hunger flooded his senses. Hunger and tempting questions. What would her skin taste like? The sweet weight of her breast? What would it feel like to have her nipple bead against his palm?

Torturous moments passed, and he forced his dark gaze away, forced himself to open the book.

"So, where are we?" she asked, settling against him.

"Chapter five," he practically growled.

It wasn't even a half hour later when he felt her head fall against his shoulder, her breathing grow even and soft. And he was thankful for the sight.

Dan picked her up and carried her into the bedroom. Pulling the covers back, he eased her onto his bed, placed the sheet back over her, then dropped into the old rocking chair.

The moonlight washed over her porcelain skin, long lashes and irresistible mouth. The bruise on her forehead was turning a purplish color, but it didn't detract from her beauty. He imagined that nothing could.

Dan leaned back in the chair, let his legs straighten, ankles cross. He'd just watch her for a few minutes; make sure she didn't wake up in a panic with visions of the accident. He had promised to protect her, after all.

But after a few minutes, his eyes drifted closed.

Five

Angel stood on the weathered porch, readying herself for the trek to town. To her right, the sun inched up over the mountains, butter-yellow with flecks of pure white. And for a moment she stopped assembling her pack and watched as God ushered in the day.

The bruise above her eyebrow twitched, no pain, just a slight tightening of the skin, but it was enough to make her think, make her wonder…

Her eyes dropped closed. And in that brief moment, she saw another set of mountains. These were not gold with morning sun but shrouded in thick fog. She felt connected to the vision, though strangely forlorn, as though she'd spied the view a thousand times with an unrequited longing in her heart.

The emotion the image evoked rattled her mind. So

much so that her eyes flew open, breaking the spell all together.

What had she seen?

Was it her home? A favorite holiday destination? A childhood haunt?

And why had she experienced such a strong sense of longing with it?

The sun illuminated the landscape as it ascended toward full glory. But its colossal radiance cast no light, no answers to her queries.

Just more questions.

But whatever the images of a fog-drenched mountain and feelings of loneliness had been, she now knew that the possibility of her memory returning was within her grasp.

Angel waited for a surge of happiness, of relief to fill her blood. But oddly, she felt only a slight twinge of wonder.

Nothing more.

She shivered. Could it be that her past was so horrible, so lonely that she wished to forget it? She swallowed thickly. Or was it that her present intrigued and excited her so much that she only wished to look forward?

"Rancon's fed and watered, has plenty of oats and hay to last him a day. All set, Angel?"

She turned sharply, caught sight of her "present" walking out the door, pack and bedroll already strapped to his back. Her gaze moved over her protector. Ruggedly handsome in hiking boots, jeans, T-shirt and blue flannel shirt, Dan looked ready for anything.

Her gaze dropped to the waistband of his jeans.

Including danger.

She walked over to him. "Is that a gun in your pants or—"

"Please don't finish that sentence," he interrupted, eyebrow rising.

"What do you mean?"

He looked at her, realized she was serious and uttered a very dry, "Nothing."

She asked again, "You have a gun, Dan?"

"Yes."

A trickle of anxiety melted through her. "You feel you need to bring protection on this trip?"

Something dark but decidedly hot flashed across his face. It was gone in an instant.

"This trip, and every trip." He whipped out the deadly black object from his waistband and placed it in his leather shoulder holster. "She goes wherever I go."

"She?" Angel asked, surprised.

"Quick, smooth and lethal." Sensuality lit his eyes, his palm grazing over the gun. "Definitely a she."

Heat flowed into her belly, then surged downward. In her mind's eye, she saw his hand, that same hand that caressed a deadly weapon, moving over her skin, making it hot and tight.

Shame filled her at such a wanton reaction, but she managed a crisp smile and a quip. "I think I'm insulted."

Dan chuckled. "You shouldn't be. It was a compliment. I'd be a fool to deny the many powers of a woman."

"Power is one thing, but you used the word *lethal*. Perhaps you mean lethal to the heart."

"To the head," he corrected, eyes locked on her. "With the right woman—or the wrong one, depending on how you look at it—a man can easily lose his mind."

Shimmers of electricity moved between them as they stood close. Angel's breath quickened, her knees softened at the clean scent of him, and far more deadly, the call of those lips beckoned her.

If she moved, reached out and touched him, how would he react? Would his hand inch for his weapon out of instinct or would he allow her access to whatever ripple of muscle, V of crisp hair, angle of sharp cheekbone she wanted to explore?

Around her a warm summer breeze sighed, echoing the new and overwhelming urge inside her.

"You ready to go, Angel?"

Need and heat disappeared at the less-than-subtle nudge into reality. Her heart dropped a few meters as she forced a nod. After all, what else could she do? Tell him, "No I'm not ready—to go to town or to find out the truth about who I am?" Could she tell him that she wanted to stay here until her memory returned? Could she tell him that being with him, around him, she felt protected and intrigued and strangely alive, and she didn't want to be rid of such wondrous feelings?

With solemn eyes, she watched Dan look over her pack, checking the zippers, the weight.

Of course she couldn't tell him any of those things. He'd made it clear that he didn't want company, especially a lost little lamb with no memory.

So she held her tongue and allowed Dan to position the small pack on her back, tried not to shiver when his fingers grazed her skin.

"Too heavy?" he asked, his breath tickling her ear.

She shook her head. "Not at all."

At breakfast, he'd insisted on carrying ninety percent of the load. She'd tried to tell him that she could handle more. But he wouldn't listen.

Dan was a stubborn, dangerous and heart-stoppingly sexy loner. And God help her, she wanted all of him.

Her spirits sank into the rough wooden planks of the deck.

After tomorrow, she'd never see him again.

"Are you sure you're up for this?" he asked her for the third time that morning.

Angel forced herself to nod, knowing darn well that he was talking about the hike, not about leaving the cabin, leaving him. "I'm sure."

The beauty of the woods was almost overwhelming. Angel followed Dan down a thin trail lined with pine and aspen, two vastly different trees that grew together like fraternal twins. The late-afternoon sunlight bobbed and flashed through their branches, giving the sensation of another hiker on the trail merrily following behind them, while their vocal sister, the wind, lapped at every leaf, every needle, mixing their scents with true artful flair.

"How are you doing?" Dan asked, glancing over his shoulder.

Angel grimaced. "I think every muscle I have is sore. And those peanut butter sandwiches from lunch? I believe they've taken me about as far as I can go."

"I hear ya," he said on a chuckle. "We'll make camp down in the valley there, by the stream."

The valley Dan led her into was like something out of a painting. Gold fields of mountain grass, red and pink flowers, a lazy river surrounded by smooth rock, and everywhere you turned, snowcapped mountains. If Dan hadn't put her to work setting up camp, she could've gazed at it forever.

While she worked, Dan built a crackling fire, then grabbed a small pole and went down to the stream to fish. Luckily for their ravishing appetites, it only took him about ten minutes to catch a large rainbow trout and another ten minutes to clean it.

And she was hoping that it would only take another ten to fry the fish. But when Dan quickly explained that he needed to wash up before dinner Angel decided to try her hand at cooking one more time. Perhaps a fish was easier than bacon and eggs. Well, at least she hoped so.

Dan was returning to camp when he encountered an all-too-familiar scent. Burned food…and something else.

He saw the something else at once. Angel was cursing and swatting out flames in the oily pan with a blanket, which had also caught fire.

Dropping his soap and towel, Dan rushed over,

grabbed the blanket and pan from her, calmly walked over the modest rise to the river's edge and dumped them both in. Angel came up beside him and sighed.

Dan glanced over at her. "So, you tried cooking the fish?"

"Perhaps."

He gestured toward the pan, soaking between two rocks. "I sure smelled it, but I didn't see it in the pan. Where is it?"

She bit her lip. "Gone."

"Gone where?"

She whirled on him, her eyes a violet storm. "It disintegrated."

She looked so angry over the stupid fish, a grin threatened to ruffle his mouth. But he resisted the urge. "You and cooking, not a good combination."

She tipped up her chin. "I see that now. I was merely trying to be helpful."

"Well, get ready to be even more helpful, Angel."

"What does that mean?"

He reached down, grabbed the soggy, tattered and badly burned blanket from the river and held it up. "That means that my bed here is gone. That means, Angel, that you and I are going to be sharing to-night."

Dan had never shared a sleeping bag in his life, even unzipped and spread out. And now here he was, lying beside this beautiful, full-of-fire woman, staring up into the clear night sky, trying like hell not to think about how warm she felt or how each time she shifted positions, her soft skin brushed against him.

For years he'd been trained to seek and recover

criminals, hard-core and not at all willing to be caught. And in those years, there'd been many a time when he'd been trapped in some pretty dangerous, pretty risky situations.

But sharing a bedroll with Angel went far past risky. In fact, it had Hazardous signs all over it.

Thankfully, they'd be in town tomorrow. Because, if he had to go through this kind of sweet torture one more night, well, God help him.

"The stars are so bright. They feel so close."

Her soft, husky tone had him inhaling the crisp pine-scented night air, hoping the coolness would act like a cold shower.

It didn't.

"Do you know anything about the stars, Dan?"

"A little." Why'd she have to talk at all? Couldn't they just knock off for the night? Didn't she get that morning would come faster if they just went to sleep.

"I must've been horrid in astronomy," she said with a soft laugh. "I can't make out one star from another. Is there anything up there that you recognize?"

She wasn't going to give up. What a surprise. So, with a sigh, he pointed at a particular mass of celestial diamonds. "That's Sagitta."

"Really? Where?"

"Well, it's pretty faint. But—" he took her hand, used the index finger as a pointer "—look at those stars in a line from there to there. And then it splits off into two. See?"

"Yes, I do." Awe filled her voice. "Sagitta...what does that mean?"

"The arrow." He still held her hand, warm and small in his own.

"I wonder whose arrow it is."

"Hercules."

"And who was he hunting?"

"Some say birds, some say a woman."

"Did he catch either?"

"No. His prey was said to have gotten away."

Dan released her hand and turned onto his side to face her. He watched her as she stared up into the sky, lips parted, eyes wide and unguarded.

"I can really make out the arrow," she exclaimed. "Oh, how wonderful." She turned to look at him. "How do you know about the stars?"

He rose onto one elbow. "Too much time on my hands or something. It's just a hobby."

"I don't believe you."

A muscle twitched in his cheek. This woman had an uncanny way of seeing through his pretext. He didn't like it. "It was my father."

"He loved the stars?"

"He did."

"And he taught you all about them?"

"Something like that. He was an astronomer."

"Was?"

The pain of loss crept up Dan's throat, but he pushed it back. It was the only way. It was how he dealt. "Both my parents died in a car wreck when I was a kid."

Sympathy burned in her expression. He'd seen that look many times. After his parents' deaths, and after Janice's. Bothered him then and bothered him now. He wasn't looking for anyone to feel sorry for him. That part of his life was over, gone, done. Hey, there were a lot worse situations out there. And he'd seen many of them firsthand.

"Losing both parents." She shook her head. "That must have been excruciatingly hard for a young child." Her eyes searched his, too intimate for comfort. "Where did you go? Did you have relatives?"

Her question stung, couldn't be helped. He hadn't thought about his aunt and uncle for a long time. Hadn't wanted to. What do you say about two people who weren't interested in taking care of a five-year-old boy, or getting to know the man he'd become?

The answer was, "not much."

He shook his head. "No family."

"I'm so sorry."

Turning away from her, he lay on his back, closed his eyes. "Go to sleep, Angel."

He didn't like this. He was the one who asked the questions, made others squirm. Not the other way around.

"You know something, Dan?" Angel said softly.

He exhaled heavily. "What now?"

"You always tell me to go to sleep when things get…well…"

"What?"

"Personal."

"Yeah, I guess I do."

"Why do you think that is?"

"Probably because the personal stuff is no one's business but mine." Maybe if he leaned over, covered her mouth with his own, suckled her tongue, nibbled that lush lower lip of hers, they'd both be too occupied and in too deep to ask questions, give answers or think about the past.

But she didn't give him a chance to save them from themselves. She said brusquely, "You're right. I'm sorry I was prying.'' Then turned over, muttering a soft ''Good night'' in her wake.

And when her breathing finally evened out, when he knew she'd fallen into a deep sleep, he opened his eyes and stared at the stars once again.

Deep in the eyes of her mind, Angel stared into a photograph. A live image that displayed not only fact but feeling as well. Three elegantly dressed couples, one older, two younger, with forms but no faces, sat close together on bejeweled chairs carved of gold, hands held, fingers intertwined.

They were in love.

All six.

Desperately in love. Their need, their devotion for one another tore through the photograph and ripped into her thudding heart.

Then the picture changed.

The couples remained, yet now another stood in their midst. A faceless, frightened woman who wanted only her freedom. But she would get none from them. Hands reached for her, grabbed at her. Terrified, she tried to move, to get away, but they held her where she stood.

A terrible ache pulsated through Angel. Panicked, she tried to escape the photograph, change the image, anything. But nothing worked.

Just as the others had held her captive, so did the picture.

Breathless, whimpering, she came awake, sat up. Reaching out, she snatched at the photograph, wanting to tear it into pieces. But there was nothing for her to grasp.

Nothing but blackness.

She gave a cry, her hands balling into fists. Then strong arms encircled her, pulled her in, pulled her close.

"Angel, what happened? What is it?"

Dan. His gruff baritone, laced with worry, registered in her muddled brain.

"They're after me," she cried hoarsely against his chest. "Why won't they let me go?"

"Who?" Dan asked. "Who's after you?"

"I don't know."

"What did you see?"

"I couldn't see."

"Angel, I want you to tell me all that you remember."

She shook her head, her voice shaking as strongly as the rest of her. "No. I don't want to remember. Please, just hold me."

"All right. Shhh. All right." Dan held her closer, whispered soothingly against her hair, "It's all right. You're safe. No one's going to hurt you, Angel. I swear to God."

As she melted into his powerful chest, images of the faceless beings darted across her mind. Who were they? And why were they after her?

Tremors shuddered through her. Had her dream been just a nightmare or a vision of the life she couldn't remember?

"I'm sure it was just a nightmare," Dan answered for her, but not sounding all that convinced.

"It was too real."

"I know, Angel. They feel like that, I know."

She eased away from him, just an inch or so, looked up at him. "Do you?"

Tenderness glowed from his eyes as he brushed a stray lock of hair from her face. "Yes, I do."

"Tell me. Tell me about your nightmares, Dan. Please."

A cloud of darkness moved over his face. "No."

She didn't press, just nodded. But disappointment moved through her like the breeze whipping through the mountain grass. More than anything, she wanted Dan's kinship, needed his connection, his obvious understanding. But he couldn't give it. And that yearning feeling was a strangely familiar one.

"I'm sorry, Angel." He cupped her face, leaned in and gave her a soft kiss on the forehead. "But I just can't do that."

Her skin ached for more, more heat, more touch. She glanced down, her gaze caught on his lips. "What can you do then?"

Beneath the shard of moonlight, she watched his eyes fill with a desire she felt rippling through her blood.

A delicious shudder drifted from her belly down into her core. The sensation felt so new, so strange, so welcome that she placed a hand to her stomach.

"What's wrong, Angel?"

"You," she fairly breathed.

"What?"

Her lips parted in hope, in waiting. A lady-in-waiting. "It's you. You make me feel…"

Mystification shadowed his expression. "I make you feel…"

"That's all. You make me feel." Her mind spun. She didn't know if such honesty was a good thing or a bad thing, but she didn't care. Not while he was this close to her.

With dark eyes blazing down, he leaned toward her, he found her, brushed his mouth against hers.

One soft, tender kiss.

A wisp of a moan escaped her lips. More, please more, she implored him silently, hoping that her mouth and body spoke for her. Hoping that he felt the hard peaks of her breasts pressed against his chest.

His breath hovered over her lips for just an instant. Then once again, his mouth closed over hers, sank into a kiss so bone-meltingly perfect she wanted to die, live, love. And down, inches below her belly, in a place she knew no man had ever been, she ached.

Like the flowers she'd seen on the trails that morning, she opened to him, for him, for herself, touching her tongue to his, urging him into passion.

And he followed.

Angel felt his chest, his muscles tighten against her, against her breasts as he took her deep. All she could imagine was his mouth on another spot, a wet, aching spot that only he could find.

But all thought was lost when he suddenly retreated, not all the way, but enough for her to miss him.

He grazed his teeth across her lower lip, groaned like a pained animal. "Angel."

"What?"

"I'm sorry." He backed away, his eyes near to black.

"For what?"

Without an answer, he eased out of the sleeping bag.

"Where are you going?"

"I need to get out of here," he said, his voice low

and granite-like. "Out from under this bag and onto that patch of grass over there."

"Why?"

He stood above her, his searing gaze pounding down into hers one last time. "You know why."

Her lips, her breasts, her womb burned with unfulfilled need as she watched him throw on another sweatshirt, walk over to the base of a wind-dancing aspen and lie down on the grass.

In her heart, she knew the reason, knew that tomorrow was their last day together, knew that he believed they weren't right for each other.

She had no memory, and he seemed to have too many memories.

On a sigh, she laid back down under the sleeping bag. The heat of their bodies totally spent now, the bag feeling as cold as her heart.

Six

They pulled into the smoky little town of Evergreen, Colorado, around nine-thirty the following morning, and headed straight for the doctor's office.

They'd barely spoken two words since last night, but when they took a seat in the waiting area, Dan felt compelled to say, "Don't tell the doctor that you're alone here, that you don't know me. Just say that you fell in the woods, got a small cut, headache, nausea and you can't remember anything."

Confused, she stared at him. "Why?"

Dan shook his head. Didn't she know that you never asked a man of the law that kind of question? Instinct, gut feeling. That was how you survived. Besides, that nightmare of hers was still nagging at him—as was the promise he'd made to protect her.

''I don't want the guy calling the cops just yet. Trust me, all right?''

She nodded, smiled tentatively. ''All right.''

That smile made his chest tighten, made his mind wander back to that kiss they'd shared. Where under a canvas of stars, he'd tasted what he'd ached to taste for two days, felt what he'd always wanted to feel: Angel wanting him.

He could still feel her mouth—like silk—so soft he wanted to get lost there for days. And he would've if his sense of duty hadn't kicked him in the ass. So instead of pulling her beneath him, he'd pulled away.

''Mrs. Mason?'' The nurse's call ripped Dan from his thoughts. He glanced up to see the woman staring at Angel, holding open the exam-room door. ''This way.''

Angel turned to Dan, whispered, ''Why is she calling me that?''

''It's my last name,'' he whispered back.

She sucked in a breath, whispered, ''Oh, I like that. You tell her your last name before you tell me?''

''Can we talk about this later?''

''No.''

''Look, I'm sorry for not telling you my last name, okay?''

''Fine. But why did you give it to the nurse, it's—''

''I put it down on the sheet when I checked you in,'' he whispered quickly, while, several feet away, the nurse tapped her foot with impatience. ''It's just easier that way, Angel. Now, you should—''

''But she thinks I'm your—''

''I want them all to think that. Especially if there

really is someone after you.'' He needed to do a bit of digging on his own, see if there was any truth to her dream. Sure, he wanted her to find her family, wanted her out of his hair, but like it or not, he'd vowed to protect her until then.

''Go on now,'' he told, gesturing toward the waiting nurse.

On a tense sniff, she stood up. ''You'll be back?''

''Yes.''

She smiled. ''All right.''

The nurse cleared her throat. ''If you're nervous, your husband can come in with you if you'd like, Mrs. Mason.''

Dan lifted an eyebrow at Angel. After their little encounter in the sleeping bag, he didn't think it was a good idea to see her in nothing more than a skimpy cotton gown and bare bottom. But if she wanted him there…

Before he could say a word, Angel shook her head. ''No. He has things to do. Many things. Supplies to buy.''

On his way out the door, Dan couldn't help but grin at her stuttered excuse. Obviously she'd been just as affected by that kiss as he'd been, and still was.

Outside, the summer morning was already prepping itself for a hot day. The town bustled as much as a small town could, neighbors talking to shopkeepers, kids pleading for things they wanted. Dan had been to Evergreen a few times since his boss had tossed him up into the mountains, and the place was always crawling with locals eager for supplies or a hot meal in the motel restaurant.

On his way to the store, Dan kept his ears open for gossip on the street, his eyes peeled for any posters or have-you-seen-this-girl flyers hanging around. But there was nothing. Odds were, if he was going to get any information, he'd have to ask.

The Greenjeans Market was run by a real western woman in her late sixties, plump and very talkative. She gave Dan a broad smile as he entered the store, told him that if he needed anything, Rachel was his gal.

For some bizarre reason, Dan felt this rookie impulse to just come out and ask the woman if she'd heard anything about a missing hiker or someone looking for a missing hiker. But he didn't. He chuckled at himself and started filling his plastic basket with provisions.

As the bell clanged over the front door, Dan reached down to grab a couple cans of that pasta Angel liked, then stopped, remembering that she wasn't coming back with him today.

"Good morning, madam. Do you own this store?"

"Surely do."

Dan's ears pricked up, his pulse slowed. The man sounded similar to Angel, with that burr of an accent.

Cautiously, Dan stood, his eyes on the can of pasta, pretending to read the label. But his gaze flickered. Two males with slicked-back dark hair, both real big and real ugly, loomed over the counter. They obviously didn't give a damn about a disguise because they weren't dressed even remotely like locals. Dan's gaze moved over their finely tailored suits and the bulges in the back.

Why the hell were they carrying?

Instinctively, Dan brushed his elbow against his gun.

"My daughter is missing," goon number one stated. "I am desperate to find her."

"Oh, my. Well, that's just awful." No doubt Rachel was making some overly sympathetic face, but Dan didn't waste any time looking at her.

"We miss her terribly," Goon One offered.

"Of course you do. How long she been gone did you say?"

Goon number two must've been a mute, because his buddy was doing all the talking. "It's been several days."

"Well, I know most of the gals that come in here. Do you have a picture?"

The man took a photograph out of his pocket, placed it on the counter. "Do you recognize this woman?"

As Rachel studied the photograph, Goon Two glanced in Dan's direction, his eyes narrowed.

Take it easy, buddy. Not going to bust you just yet.

Nice and slow, Dan tossed the can of pasta in his basket, grabbed a loaf of bread and headed up to the counter.

Rachel was shaking her head woefully. "Nope, haven't seen her. But I'll keep my eye out."

Dan dropped his basket on the counter, checking out the picture in the process. A smiling Angel stared up at him. Until now, he hadn't been convinced that these guys were after her or that her dream of being chased was anything more than a nightmare. His elbow grazed his Glock once again.

Goon One nodded in his direction. "Have you seen this woman, sir?"

His hands itching to fist, Dan shook his head. "Sorry. Sure pretty though."

The man's already thin lips practically disappeared under his teeth—teeth Dan would have no problem knocking out, one at a time while the guy confessed. But Dan didn't do a thing and Goon One turned away, slipped a card on the counter for the clerk. "If you see her."

Rachel nodded pleasantly. "Sure thing, mister."

When the men left, Dan followed them, grabbing some beef jerky by the door as he memorized the plate number of their long, silver car.

"Strange fellers," Rachel commented when he returned to the counter.

"I'd say so. They staying in town?"

"Looks like it. They left the number of the Evergreen Motel."

Dan was about to ask for the room number, but he stopped himself. He couldn't get sloppy now, or raise any gossip or suspicion.

No worries. His buddy at the FBI would find out the truth. Right now Dan needed to get back to the doctor's office before anyone else saw Angel.

"Besides the small cut, which has healed rather nicely, I see nothing physically wrong with you."

Spine straight, Angel sat in the doctor's office, fully dressed now, and asked the question that had been on her mind since she'd woken up in Dan's bed, the question this doctor had yet to address. "Doctor, in cases like this, how soon do patients recall their...well, their lives, their past."

He nodded sympathetically. "I understand your impatience, Mrs. Mason."

Unbidden, her heart shifted, pinged, just as it had every time the doctor had referred to her as Dan's wife.

"It must be very frustrating," he said with a gentle smile. "Give it a little time, another week, to return naturally, then come and see me again."

A week, Angel thought anxiously. What was she going to do for a whole week? Alone? In a strange town—in a strange world. Perhaps she should tell the doctor the truth, that Dan wasn't her husband, that he didn't even know her, and that perhaps he should call someone who could find her real family.

Trust me, Angel.

She swallowed thickly as Dan's words seeped into her muddled brain. The truth was, she did trust him. But the truth was, he wasn't offering to let her stay.

"The man who brought you in is Mr. Mason, your husband, correct?"

Angel looked up, startled. "Excuse me?"

"The man who brought you here? He's your husband?"

"He is Mr. Mason, yes." Lying did not come easily to her, and she hoped the man didn't press her further.

But hoping can lead to disappointment. Maybe even embarrassment. The doctor was frowning at her, as though she were one of his grandchildren, hand caught in the cookie jar, so to speak. "And what are you and your husband doing up here in the mountains? You don't live in the area, do you?"

She swallowed thickly. "No."

"With the head injury, perhaps I should call the sheriff. Perhaps there's a report to fill out. Just as a precautionary measure, of course—"

Behind her, Angel heard the husky baritone of her "husband." "Can I come in?"

"Of course, Mr. Mason." The doctor waved Dan inside. "We're just wrapping things up."

Dan walked to her, put his hand on her shoulder, squeezed reassuringly. Her skin tingled, warmed at his touch, and she leaned into his side.

"So, Doc, is my wife going to be all right?"

Angel watched the older man size Dan up. "She's perfectly fine, except for the memory loss."

Dan sighed. "I can't believe this happened. And on our honeymoon and everything."

"Honeymoon?" the doctor asked, eyes wide. "Well, my goodness. Why didn't you tell me about this, young lady?"

A smile broke out on Angel's face, but inside she was sinking. The doctor would release her now, Dan would return to the cabin and she would just wander around Evergreen, Colorado, until her memory came back. "I was about to tell you, when my husband walked in."

A wide, understanding, accepting smile took the place of the doctor's frown. "Goodness, newlyweds.

Must be something awful not remembering your past together."

Dan kissed her on the cheek. "We're making new memories, aren't we, Angel?"

She glanced up at him. He grinned down at her as though he hadn't a care in the world. But she could tell something was wrong. He looked pensive and ready to spring.

The doctor winked at Dan. "She just needs plenty of rest and relaxation, son, and it'll all come back. I'm certain of it."

As Angel stood up, Dan took her hand. "That's wonderful. See, honey, what did I tell you?"

"Bring her back in a week," the doctor said, his hand extended.

Dan shook the man's hand. "Thank you, Doctor. Will do."

Once outside, Dan leaned close to her ear and whispered, "Walk quickly."

"But, you should know—"

"Not now," he insisted. "Come with me."

They moved as swiftly as they could with their heavy gear, slowing whenever they passed a townsperson. Finally, when they reached the outskirts of town, he let her stop, catch her breath.

"Where are we going?" she asked.

"Back to the cabin."

"I don't understand. What's going on, Dan?"

He glanced around, his jaw tight. "There's no time to explain. If you're okay, we need to get the hell out of here." He tugged on her hand, but she held her ground.

"You were planning on leaving me in town and now you're taking me back to the cabin. You need to tell me why."

He released her hand, exhaled. "That dream you had last night was no dream at all. Someone's after you."

The words went in, knocked about her in her chest, then slowly gripped her heart. "Say that again."

"Someone's after you, Angel."

"How do you know?"

"I saw them."

"Them?"

"Two. Real Euro dirtbags."

"European." Out of nowhere, a flash of two dark-eyed, dark-haired beings erupted in her mind. She blinked, uttered, "Big men?"

His eyes widened with alarm. "Yes. Are you remembering something else? Do you know who these guys are? Where they're from and—"

"Dan, please." She gave a frustrated, weary shrug, the image totally gone. Dark confusion swept over her, but she fought to keep her wits about her. "How do you know that these men are after me?"

"They were showing your picture around, asking questions—"

"Well, that doesn't mean that they're after me," she argued. "They could be my family, or friends of the family."

"They're not."

"How do you know?" she implored.

Around them, the wind picked up, sending pine needles and leaves into the air. One clipped Dan on the jaw, his rigid jaw. "I'm a cop, okay, Angel. A U.S. marshal. I can detect trouble a mile away. Those guys weren't family or friends. And you damn well know it, too!"

Between all the dreams and realities, she felt so tired and confused, she wasn't sure what she knew. "Dan, you've done enough for me. If there's a problem here, you don't need to take it on."

He took her hand again, passed his thumb over her palm. "Yeah, I do."

"I'm sure the police can handle—"

"No."

Why was she fighting this? She wanted to be with him, near him, under his wing of protection. Weariness and need answered for her. "All right. What do we do?"

"We head back to the cabin." With one last glance toward town, Dan pulled her with him into the shelter of the forest.

Deep in the mountains, Angel sat on a dead log, her arms hugging her chest, small trembles of worry running up and down her spine as the situation she found herself in finally settled.

Someone was after her.

Two someones, in fact. And she had no clue who they were or what they wanted from her. The only thing she did sense was the powerful need she had to elude them.

Above her, the sky turned cobalt as afternoon aged. Soon, it would be night. A shiver moved over her skin. When she went to sleep tonight, would she dream of her past, of the men who searched for her? When she went to sleep tonight, would Dan be beside her this time, protecting her, keeping her warm?

Her stomach growled comically in response, hunger suddenly overtaking fear. She and Dan had eaten their lunch on the trail, on the move, not stopping, just walking until he'd felt they were far enough away from town. No doubt if he'd have thought Angel up to it, he'd have pushed her to get back to the cabin, by the light of the moon and his darling stars, no less.

A sigh escaped her lips and she leaned toward the fire. The worry, the fear, they were understandable emotions for someone to have at a time like this. But oddly, they weren't the only emotions that ran through her.

She felt relief and satisfaction, as well.

Yesterday morning, she'd wanted nothing more than to stay in the cabin with Dan. Now, because of the men who searched for her, she was granted that wish.

The odd shiver returned to her skin, but whether it was from the day's worry or the future's wonder, she wasn't sure.

"You okay, Angel?"

Over her shoulder, she smiled grimly. "Not really."

Abandoning the food he was hastily unpacking, he came over, dropped down beside her on the log. "Everything's going to be okay."

"I hope you're right."

"What happened to trusting me?"

She couldn't halt the gentle roll of laughter that

escaped her throat. "Trust you? You didn't even tell me who you were until today."

"I told you my name."

"First name," she corrected. "But that was it."

"There was no reason for you to know who I am until today."

"Of course there was."

"Why is that?"

"Because…well…" Her tongue refused to cooperate. She couldn't say it. She wasn't going to bring up that kiss, that unbelievably amazing kiss, and how the intimacy of it demanded his full disclosure. He wouldn't understand that reasoning. After all, it had been just a passing fancy, a mistake to him. She turned back to the fire. "Forget it."

"Angel…"

He touched her shoulder. Again, the shiver returned.

She shook her head. "I don't know why, but I can't seem to get warm."

"You're worn out, that's all."

"I'm fine."

With a gentle touch, he snaked an arm around her waist, helped her to her feet. "Come with me. I want to show you something."

Thirty seconds later they stood in front of a kidney-shaped hot spring tucked away in a verdant cove. Angel stared in wonderment, in disbelief of the wild loveliness that was laid out before her. Cords of vine wound around the white trucks of an aspen, then dipped into the water and were lost from view. Smooth rock circumscribed the pool, while delicious steam rose off the water's surface, welcoming those who needed a good soak.

Angel's shoulders fell at the sight as though it were too good to be true.

"Is this a mirage?"

Beside her, Dan chuckled. "No."

"A dream?"

"Nope. In fact, I stopped here on my way back to the cabin on my last trip into town and took a dip, so I know it's real."

A scattering of blue flowers floated past on an exceptionally clear ripple. "Oh, how lovely."

"You take a nice long soak. Camp's within earshot. Just call if there's a problem." He turned and walked away.

"But I don't have a suit," she called after him.

He glanced over his shoulder, eyebrow raised, eyes ripe with amusement. "You don't need one, Angel."

Heat surged into her cheeks and she laughed. "Oh, of course."

"I'll leave you to it then." He lingered for just a moment before he turned and walked away.

When he was gone, when his footsteps diminished and left only the music of the mountains, crickets, water lapping and the wind rushing through the trees, she peeled off one piece of clothing at a time.

Finally, when she was completely bare and her hair hung loose, she took a deep breath and stepped down into the steamy water.

Every inch of her sighed as liquid heat rushed through her blood.

Pure heaven, she mused as she sat down on a

smooth stone that was settled into the bottom of the pool. With a satisfied smile, she tilted her head back, let the water lap at the tops of her breasts, let her hair splay over the bank, let her thoughts and fears go.

Time passed in whispered waves, her mind a welcome blank canvas. But like any canvas, it soon begged to be painted.

Sudden rushes of image flickered behind her closed lids. First she only heard music, classical and so familiar. She saw herself garbed in a long, flowing ball gown of silver, dancing with an older man.

Then the image shifted abruptly; ocean waves lapped against her feet. She sat on a warm sandy beach as the sun set peach and cherry. Her body was perfectly content, but her heart was empty as a cave.

Slightly panicked, she looked around her. There was no one on the beach. There was no love in her heart.

Behind her came a crash of noise and action. She whirled to see a mass of people, photographers and townsfolk descending upon her like ants with an extra-large crumb in sight.

Then something wet and slimy landed on her chest, and everything dissolved.

Angel gasped, eyes slamming open.

She stared at the massive frog perched on her chest. It croaked at her.

She squealed, jumped up, flicked the slimy creature off her chest and back into the water where it belonged.

"Angel?" Dan came bounding out of the woods, gun drawn. His expression fierce, highly alert, he stood at the very edge of the pool, only a few feet from her, ready to do battle. "What the hell happened? Are you all right?"

"Frog," she managed to say between shallow gasps.

"What?"

"A frog…jumped on my…my chest."

His gaze slipped downward.

"Angel?"

"What?"

He was as calm and as cool as the ball of moon in the twilit sky. "Not that I'm complaining, but you know you're only wearing a few drops of water, right?"

The flame that licked his dark orbs moved through her as well, that is, until the meaning of what he'd just said slammed into her.

She glanced down at her nude body, gave a horrified squeak, then dropped back into the water.

Seven

Had he died and gone to heaven?

Or was it hell?

Dan shoved his gun back in the waistband of his jeans. When he turned around, Angel had swum a few feet away from him. She was now backed against the rock wall, hair wet, eyes large and bright, the tops of her breasts raising and lowering with each weighty breath she took.

But it didn't matter that she was safely huddled below the water or that night was coming on fast or that when he'd first seen her, the water had just grazed her midthigh. No. The image of her—creamy skin, long legs, small, perfect breasts, tiny waist and the kind of curvy hips that made a man desperate to take them between his hands—was permanently tattooed on his weakening brain.

"Are you going to say something, Dan?"

"I'm working on it," he said, his voice low, gruff.

She groaned. "I think I'm embarrassed."

"What do you mean, you think?"

"Let's just say I have the distinct feeling I've never been naked in front of a man before."

His chest tightened almost to the point of pain. How was that possible? She had to be around twenty-five years old. Oh, but if it was possible…if no man had seen her without clothes, why did he have to be the first?

Pure, delicious torture.

Through gritted teeth, he muttered, "You have absolutely no reason to be embarrassed, Angel."

She looked hopeful. "You mean, because it was too dark for you to see me?"

He shook his head, the vision of her burning through his brain once again. "No, I saw you."

"Great."

"You were showing off the early moonlight to mouth-dropping perfection. That's all I meant." He was turning into a flesh-and-blood man right in front of her. And that fact really pissed him off.

He'd lost the battle over control. Like a randy teenager, he'd let her know how much he wanted her.

Couldn't take that back, and couldn't take back his vision of her either.

She shifted restlessly in the water, and as the creamy sweep of her breasts assaulted his vision, she said, "Showing off the moonlight? Is that right?"

He wanted to laugh. "You sound intrigued."

She managed an impish smile that hit him solidly

in the chest, then dropped low, painfully low. "Not intrigued. A little flattered, perhaps."

"Just a little?"

"All right. I'm very flattered."

This game was making him nuts. *She* was making him nuts. The power that this woman seemed to lord over him every time he looked at her threatened everything he'd worked so hard to build over the last four years. He couldn't allow that wall of protection to be destroyed. "Well, maybe you shouldn't be."

"Why not?"

"A man can get dangerous under a moon like this. Especially when he's being tortured by a beautiful and very naked woman."

Tentatively, she swam toward him, stopped by his feet and looked up, her eyes cautious but sincere. "I might have been a little embarrassed at you seeing me...bare but I'd never be afraid of you, Dan."

"You should be afraid." Especially if she stayed right where she was, with that need his body understood glowing in her violet eyes.

She sat back, frowning. "Why do you talk like that, say things like that? You're protecting me, aren't you?"

Instantly, his elbow drew back, scuffed the butt of his weapon. Of course he was protecting her. In fact, he'd run to her like a madman when he'd heard her cry out. Chest gripped by an imaginary vise, pulse hovering around two hundred.

"I'm protecting you, Angel. But not just from them." He lifted his eyebrow suggestively.

"From yourself as well, right?" She sounded curt, frustrated.

"That's right."

"And if I get involved with you…"

Shaking his head, he said vehemently, "That's not going to happen."

He waited for a why but it didn't come. Instead, she asked, "That's not going to happen with me, or with anyone?"

He attempted to answer her question without words. Not because the impact would be stronger, but because his throat felt as tight as the rest of him.

She wasn't appeased by his silent reply. "What are you so afraid of Dan?"

He was used to this query, from criminals, skips, addicts. They tried to cause problems, see if they could trigger something, get you to drop your guard and make a mistake.

Never worked. Hadn't in the past anyway.

But with Angel it worked like a bullet to the heart. Probably because the question was wrapped up in desire and a need he hadn't felt in a long time.

He shook his head. "This isn't about fear."

"What is it about then?"

"Finding out who you are so you can go back to your life and—"

"And get out of yours," she finished for him.

He didn't say a word.

Slowly, she nodded. "I get it."

The hell she did. But he wasn't going to enlighten her. Angel was a good woman, open and honest, not afraid to speak her mind, ask for what she wanted.

But in this, wanting him, she was foolish. He was here to protect her. That was it. Besides his world was no place for a woman like her—or any woman—but especially someone like her.

If she'd just wait it out, wait until her memory returned, maybe there was a real stand-up guy, a doctor maybe, a real hero, waiting for her.

Not some messed-up marshal with a chip on his shoulder the size of Colorado.

"Food's ready." He pushed off the rock wall. "Why don't you dry off, get dressed and come back to camp."

As he stalked away, he heard her step out of the water, heard the rustling of clothing. Flashes of pink skin, wet and smooth, erupted in his brain.

He cursed, kicked a rock out of his way, while the lower half of him growled to life with a want he refused to fulfill.

Angel lay on her back under the sleeping bag, the strong press of Dan's thigh against hers, the spicy scent that clung to his skin invading her senses and the heat that he exuded calming, yet thrilling her blood.

Tonight, she wasn't going to be without him.

After dinner, she'd told him that she didn't want to sleep alone, that she was afraid of the men who were after her. That was a reasonable excuse to have him in her bed. She *was* afraid. But the driving force behind the request was her want to have him close, his warmth and strength suffusing her.

And if he happened to pull her close and kiss her

again, perhaps touch her, minister to all those aching spots he'd awakened in her, she'd willingly comply.

In her heart, she knew his reluctance didn't have as much to do with her memory loss and unclaimed past as he'd tried to make her believe.

Something else held him back, not just from taking what she offered, but from taking what life offered. A fear, perhaps even an unclaimed past of his own that he refused to acknowledge.

Beside her, Dan shifted, scratched his left arm, brushing the underside of her breast in his haste. Her breath caught in her throat as that deep, electric heat that knew Dan by name roused to life.

"Sorry about that," he whispered.

"It's okay."

"You have enough to eat?"

Gruff and wary, he still managed to show his care for her welfare and comfort at every turn.

"Yes. And thank you for making dinner."

"It was just that canned spaghetti you like. No biggie."

"Chef Buoyancy?"

A deep chuckle rippled through the cool, night air. "Chef Boyardee."

"Right." She turned on her side, a thought flickering in her mind. "We didn't pack any canned food, did we?"

He stared straight up into the heavens, into the stars he knew so intimately. "No, we didn't."

"Did you get it at the store this morning?"

"I guess so."

Her mouth curved with tenderness. "That was very thoughtful of you."

"Just practical, Angel."

"How do you figure?"

"Canned pasta's pretty hard to burn." He glanced over at her, his eyes alight with humor.

Her smile turned to laughter. She cuffed him on the arm. "You just wait. I'm going to master the art of cooking. Then you'll be begging me to make you dinner."

"I don't beg for anything."

She had no idea where the impulse came from, but she reached out and lightly pinched the side of his taut stomach.

He jumped, then looked over at her, warning in his eyes. "Don't even think about it."

She grinned. "I must have been a real troublemaker in my previous life, because I'm going to do more than think about it."

And with that, she let her hands go, let her fingers tickle and torture and squeeze ruthlessly. As he jumped and cursed and gave in to a moment of laughter, she called out merrily, "I can't believe the big, bad U.S. marshal is ticklish."

Before the last word left her lips, Dan gripped one of her wrists in his hand. "You try that again and I won't be responsible for what happens."

Her body aroused and her good sense all but gone, she asked, "What'll happen, Deputy?"

His eyes glowed. "I'm warning you, don't get curious."

With her heart pounding an erratic rhythm, she

gave him a bold smile, lowered her free hand to his thigh and squeezed.

She felt the jolt that rippled through him.

He had her on her back in seconds, had her arms pinned over her head, his eyes burning down into hers. "Now look what you've made me go and do."

All amusement swiftly died as she felt his erection against her stomach. She couldn't think, couldn't move. Could only want.

"Kiss me, Dan."

As if she were made of fire and had scorched him, he released her hands. "What?"

"Kiss me," she repeated, her tone husky appeal. "Not soft like last night, but hard."

"You're out of your mind."

"I know." Arching against him, she trailed her fingers up his bare back. "Let's both be out of our minds."

He shuddered. "Angel, don't you get it? You don't even know who you are, who you belong to, who—"

"I belong to no one—not in the way you mean."

"How do you know that?"

She thought of every dream, every flash of memory she'd had since her fall. She thought of her reaction to Dan's glances, his touch, the newness of this need she felt whenever they were near, and she answered him in all honesty, *"I know."*

He glanced up toward the stars, released a breath, then returned to her. "Why is it so hard to resist you?"

She lifted her head and pressed a kiss to his lips, murmured, "Perhaps because you're not meant to."

His hands plunged into her hair, fisted. "God help us both."

She wrapped her arms around him as his mouth came down on hers, branding her, claiming her. Blood pounding in her veins, she opened to him, tasted him. He wasn't gentle. He was what she wanted him to be; ravenous.

Yet, she knew he held back. Though his need and want and feeling were all there in his kiss and touch, his heart remained aloof.

All while she soared and gave.

Hot, wet mouth against mouth, he released her hair, let his hand fall. Slipping under her sweatshirt, he cupped her breast.

Moaning, throaty and on the edge, she pressed herself into his palm. She wanted to tell him again that this was new, that no one had touched her like this, but she was afraid to break the spell. She didn't need words, his or hers, not now. She needed action.

Dan kissed her mouth, kneaded her flesh like a man dying of thirst. She didn't know what had kept him from drinking, but she was here to fill him as he filled her.

She gripped the muscles of his back as he flicked her hardened nipple with his thumb, back and forth. Then he took the peak between his thumb and forefinger and gently squeezed.

Shudders of heat and shocking electric waves pulsed in her womb. How could such feeling start in one place and move to every inch inside and out so quickly? she wondered, pressing her hips up, hoping he heard her silent cry.

She ached for him to slip inside her, arousal or hand, it didn't matter at this point. The connection was all that mattered.

Her shaky, fumbling fingers found the waistband of her sweatpants. She started to pull them down, down.

Dan froze when the softness of her hot abdomen met the steel length of him. In the middle of blistering desire and a feeling so amazing he wanted to howl, he forced his mind to return. He was an idiot. How could he get to this point, take them both to this point without a thought to the outcome?

He rolled off her. Then sat, palm to forehead.

He felt her hand on his back, heard her soft voice rip into his heart. "What's wrong?"

Any excuse was the right one at this point. "I don't have any protection."

The double meaning in those words hit him fist to gut. Truth was, with her, he was starting to feel all the anger, all the grief that had been festering within him for four years, start to subside, a feat that knocking around that dirtbag skip hadn't even accomplished.

Why did she have to have this effect on him? Why her? Why couldn't she understand that he didn't want to feel anything? Cold and empty had served him well.

Cold and empty had stopped him from giving her any kind of pleasure tonight.

His hands formed fists. If he heard her moan one

more time, felt her mouth, tasted her skin, he was afraid of what would happen to him both physically and otherwise.

He turned, looked down into those fire-filled orbs of hers and felt himself slipping. He couldn't care less about his own gratification, he wanted to touch her, wanted to hear her scream his name as she took her pleasure. But he wouldn't allow one more link to be tied between them.

Jaw as tight as his groin, he laid down beside her, whispered a hoarse, "Come here," then pulled her into his arms and held her painfully close.

She would have the closeness she craved and he, the sinking torture he was used to, and sadly all too comfortable in.

The afternoon sun was swallowing up the mountains by the time they reached the cabin the following day. After they'd checked on Rancon, Angel volunteered to feed, water and brush down the horse while Dan put away the packs and supplies. Dan had readily agreed, which made Angel wonder if perhaps he needed to gain some distance.

After all, they'd spent all night in each other's arms and all day side by side on the trail. How many times had he proved that he was a loner, enjoyed his peace, quiet and solitude? And then there was the fact that he wanted her and was fighting it at every turn.

There was no arrogance in this assumption.

Angel had seen the truth in his eyes last night, just as she'd stripped her own need bare for him to see.

With a sad little smile affixed to her lips, Angel

went about her work, feeding and watering Rancon, trying to focus her attention and thought on the nurse and not on his master. Until her gaze caught on a small tape deck hanging from a peg on the stable wall.

Feeling a surge for a little pick-me-up, she went over to it and pushed play. A man's husky singing voice burst through the small speakers in a crystal-clear twang. Just as she'd hoped, the soulful music soothed her weary bones, lifted her spirits.

Why didn't Dan understand that she wanted nothing from him, no more than he could give? She picked up a brush and went to work on Rancon's black coat with long, even strokes. Perhaps because she hadn't told Dan what she wanted and didn't want, just as she hadn't told him that she was swiftly falling in love with him.

Her heart dipped at the silent admission. The same heart that now belonged to Dan Mason, deputy U.S. marshal. She'd never been in love, and she knew it as surely as she knew she'd been around horses for most of her life and adored chocolate.

Some things even a lost memory couldn't mask. But how long could she keep from telling Dan? And if she did tell him, how would he react? Would he push her away again?

Beside her, the horse snorted as if hearing her thoughts.

Angel laughed. "Your master is a very stubborn man, Rancon."

"He knows."

Whirling around, she spied Dan in the doorway.

She grimaced at him. "Does he also know how sneaky you are?"

"Never heard him call me sneaky."

"How about full-of-it?"

"Now, that one rings a bell."

She grinned. "By the way, was the 'stubborn' comment all you heard me say to Rancon?"

"Yep."

"Good to know." And she meant it. For the life of her, she couldn't recall if she'd voiced any of those heartfelt admissions aloud.

Pushing away from the wall, Dan walked over, gave Rancon a pat on the withers. "What kind of rumors is she spreading, boy?"

"He won't tell you."

Mock disappointment coated Dan's features as he shook his head at the horse. "Falling under the spell of a woman. How many times have we talked about this?"

"Not enough, apparently. It didn't take much convincing for him to agree to keep my secrets."

"No?"

She shook her head, big smile playing about her lips. "Three carrots and a kiss."

"Can I get in on that deal?"

A softness played in her belly. "Only if you promise to keep my secrets."

"All right."

She wanted to, but the words refused to come. Instead of "I'm falling in love with you," she went safe and lackluster, "I love this music."

Dan patted Rancon again. Pouring out of the tape

deck came a love song, crooned in rough and rugged sensuality.

"You dance?" he asked.

Her hand tightened around the brush. "Me or Rancon?"

The look he tossed her way had her heart stumbling. "You, Angel."

"You mean with a partner?"

"That's what I mean."

He took the brush from her, dropped it into the tack box, then snaked an arm around her waist. Gingerly, she placed a hand in his, the other one on his shoulder.

Slowly, they moved together to the music, Dan leading the way. He was a wonderful dancer, holding her so close, his movement confident. But as the song swelled with feeling, as Dan drew her closer—her belly nestled against his arousal, her breasts, tight and aching brushing his chest—his eyes filled once again with the need she so desperately wanted to satisfy.

Instinctively, she'd watched another couple dancing this way, felt a grave longing to have what they had, feel what they were feeling.

She brushed away the vision and smiled up at him. "I guess I dance."

The smile he returned was hard. "Angel?"

"What?"

"I'm heading back into town tomorrow."

A flicker of apprehension, of loss, coursed through her. "To do what?"

"Ask some questions, run a license plate, talk to a buddy of mine at the FBI."

She hated the drop of her heart, the immediate surge of loneliness. "And you want to go alone?"

"I can get in and out fast."

She nodded, stopped dancing, pulled away.

"It's safer for you here, Angel," he explained tightly.

"For me or for you?"

"Don't start this—"

"It's started. In fact, it's a few days past the starting line."

His face hardened. "Yeah, I guess you're right about that."

She straightened, pointed a finger at him. "I *am* right. And you know what else? You don't trust yourself around me."

"Damn right I don't," he returned hotly.

For a good minute they stared at one another. Tempers up, blood flowing hot. What could she say now? How could she keep fighting, reaching for him when he didn't want to be caught?

Weariness crept into her heart. She'd had enough tonight. Her voice calm, she said, "I'm going to get washed up and go to bed." And without a glance in his direction, she turned on her heel and left the barn.

Eight

"**S**he's around five-six, a hundred twenty pounds. Long, light-brown curly hair with streaks of blond and red kind of running through it. Oh, and violet eyes."

As Dan leaned back against the wall of the phone booth, his FBI buddy, Jack Bonner, chuckled. "Violet eyes, huh?"

"That's right."

"And light-brown curly hair with red and blond streaks, you say?"

"Are you repeating this for yourself or to piss me off?" Dan ground out, ready to reach through the phone and pummel his friend.

Jack chuckled. "To piss you off, and to amuse myself."

They'd known each other for over ten years, even

started out in the police academy together. Called the
maverick men by the other cops because of their un-
conventional ways of hunting a suspect, they'd
formed a quick bond.

But the title of police officer hadn't fit either one
of them, and after a few years Jack had ditched the
force for the FBI, while Dan went into the marshals'
service.

To the surprise of some, their friendship had en-
dured. Sure, they regularly gave each other a hard
time—shoot, had to—but when it counted, there was
nothing they wouldn't do for each other. When a suspect had blown part of Jack's leg off, Dan had been
there, pushing him to recover and get back to work.
And when Janice had died, it had been Jack who'd
kicked Dan's butt out of bed after a month of feeling
like total hell.

"She's also got an accent," Dan told his buddy,
watching as the town rolled up their sidewalks—or
dirtwalks in this case—and packed in the day. "You
writing this stuff down?"

Jack gave a derisive snort. "Who do you think
you're talking to, Mason?"

Dan heard the muffled sound of paper being torn.
He grinned. "I was saying she has an accent."

"Southern? British? Brooklyn? What?"

"British, Scottish, Irish. Not exactly sure."

"You think she comes from money?"

"She sure acts like it. Perfect manners, perfect
speech, can't cook, crosses her ankles when she sits,
was wearing top-of-the-line boots when I found her."

"Rich girls can be a royal pain in the ass."

"Actually, that's the part that doesn't fit Angel." The moment the pet name slipped from his lips he wanted to bite it back. But he didn't get the chance.

"Angel?" Jack drawled.

Jaw tight, Dan muttered, "I had to call her something, okay?"

"That's so sweet, man."

"Up yours, Bonner." In three seconds, they were nineteen again, ribbing each other over who had the hottest car, hottest girl, hottest weapon.

"Glad to see the mountain air hasn't changed you too much, Mason." Jack chuckled. "Or maybe it's the curly-haired and very beautiful rich pain in the—"

"She's no pain in the ass, she's...well, to be honest, she's adorable."

"Adorable? You *are* gone, man."

"I swear to God, I can't wait to get out of here and—"

"Buy me a beer?"

"Try again."

"Look, buddy, in all seriousness, I'm on this." And just like that, Jack fell back into his role as federal agent—and friend. "I'll nose around, find out why those guys are driving a car with plates registered to the governor. Could be that the governor's felon brother loaned the car to some of his idiot pals. Or maybe this girl's the daughter of someone important. Either way, I'll find out. In the meantime, keep your eye on them."

The sunset blazed a path of orange fire up Main Street, the heat of it shooting into the phone booth, straight into Dan's gut. "I have a real strong feeling these are not amateurs we're dealing with."

"Yeah, I get that same feeling."

"I'll call you back in a few days."

"Sounds good. Hey, and Dan?"

"What?"

"Violet eyes? Seriously?"

Shaking his head, Dan chuckled. "After that beer, you're gonna get a serious pounding, Bonner."

"Later, buddy."

Dan leaned back against the phone booth, watched an old man and his wife go into the general store for last-minute provisions. Things were shutting down for the day, but his mind would stay open—twenty-four hours, most likely. He had some questions to ask, then a plan to make.

The options that Jack had raised about Angel's situation made him cringe. To be honest, neither one sounded all that good. She was either in some serious trouble or the kid of some major player.

Both great reasons for him to back off, ignore this insatiable need he had for her and play it safe. But he'd never liked playing it safe. And even more so now that he'd met Angel.

Dan slammed his fist into the phone booth's Plexiglas wall. He didn't miss women, for chrissakes. He saw them when he saw them.

But even as he thought, made excuses, tried to push her out of his mind, she remained, all violet eyes and long curly hair, all open honesty and willingness to try and fail. His body flexed, so did his mind.

He'd be back with her by sunset tomorrow. Dan

stalked out of the phone booth. Tonight, he had work
to do.

Brushing his arm against the concealed weapon at
his side, he headed toward the hotel for a T-bone
steak and a side or two of information.

On a groan of discontent, Angel dumped what was
supposed to be a cherry pie into the garbage and returned to the countertop with the empty pie plate and
a growing sense of determination to prove that she
could cook, prove that she had one ounce of domes-
ticity in her body.

Practice, that was all it took.

It was close to 9:00 p.m. She'd practiced for five
hours now and she'd managed a decent strip or two
of bacon without incident. But bacon wasn't enough.

By the time Dan returned tomorrow night, she
wanted to present him with a real meal, totally edible,
no black topping or smoke plumes.

And if the fates were with her, the meal might actually look pretty, too.

After cutting the shortening—a phrase she'd had to
look up in the back of a cookbook—into the flour and
adding cold water, she rolled the all-new piecrust into
a ball, then put it in the minifridge. Yes indeed, she
was going to serve him a great meal, a great meal
provided by a temptress.

A thoughtful grin curved her mouth. She knew she
was no temptress, had little experience in that area
anyway, but she was going to do her best. Something
told her that time was growing short, both in memory
and location. Before she had to leave, she would show

Dan how she felt about him, show him how much she loved him.

She opened another can of cherries, took one and popped it in her mouth.

When she showed him, would he take what she offered? Would a man so closed off to emotion and feeling even recognize...

The tart sweetness of the cherry suddenly burst on her tongue. Something flashed before her. Another flash, like a bolt of black lightning, shot straight into her mind.

She stumbled back, clutching her forehead, feeling the scar beneath her fingers. Gripping the side of the counter, she eased herself down onto the cool linoleum.

But the images didn't wait for her to get comfortable. They burst into her mind, one after the other. Perfect photographs, brilliant color. She was a child, sitting up on the roof of a cottage, picking cherries from a massive tree. The flower-dotted land stretched for miles, all the way to a rocky coast. Two boys sat beside her, both older, eating more cherries than they were picking, grinning like clowns at a circus. They resembled her. One had her nose, the other her eyes.

Suddenly the moving pictures added sound. Ocean slapping against rock, wind whispering through the cherry tree, boys laughing. Then someone called up to them, a woman dressed in a lavender gown, a diamond-studded tiara upon her head.

The ache of tears settled deep in Angel's throat at the sweet sound.

''Fara!'' she heard herself cry.

The woman smiled up at her. "Be more than you think possible, little lamb. Don't run away, and don't give up on love or the love of others."

Then all was gone—the land, the boys, the woman, the cherry tree—flickered out like the flames on a burner.

Angel blinked, let her lids rise. Tears fell from her eyes as she took in the familiar little cabin.

She knew that the woman in her vision was family, a mother figure. The bond was unmistakable. She knew that the land far away and by the sea was her home. But strangely, though she felt happiness, a sense of love and tradition with those people and in that place, her mind fought against knowing the truth.

Just as her body fought against being caught and returning home.

With a strength she was only beginning to realize she possessed, she stood up and returned to her work.

Before she went anywhere, remembered anything, she needed to experience the life here. Time was the answer to both her past and her future. She would have to be content with that.

When Dan returned to the cabin the following afternoon, day was drifting into night, and what had once been smoke pluming from the windows of his cabin was now an amazing aroma.

After taking Rancon, who had stopped limping, for a quick circuit around the corral, Dan trudged up the cabin steps to see the woman who had occupied his thoughts for a full forty-eight hours.

But when he opened the screen door, he paused,

watched as she took a pan out of the oven. The idea that the domestic scene was odd in any way didn't really occur to him. No doubt because his mind was gone, leaving only senses. And those were on high alert.

His gaze traveled over her. Hair piled on top of her head, no makeup, yet she was staggeringly beautiful. She wore the tank top she'd had on under her sweatshirt when they'd met and a pair of his boxers. Bare feet, long legs, tantalizing curves.

His mouth watered.

"You've been busy."

She turned with a start, then immediately smiled when she saw him. "Welcome back."

"Thanks. Good to be back." And he meant it.

On those two sexy limbs, she walked over to him, helped him take off his pack. "So, did you find out anything?"

"Not much. Have a friend working on it though. Shouldn't be too long now." Besides the fact that the world was keeping Angel's disappearance pretty quiet with no news stories and no missing person's reports that matched her description, all Dan had to go on right now was supposition.

He sure didn't need to burden her with car registration information, the fact that the two dirtbags had surveillance equipment, invisible communicators and high-tech transmitters in their motel room or that the doctor who had treated her the other day had given Dan a real strange look when they'd passed in the street this morning.

"Are those two men still in town?" she asked, unloading his pack.

He saw her hand shake, just a touch, and it made the urge to gather her in his arms almost unbearable. But he held his ground.

"Yeah, they're still there." In town, and asking questions. Actually, they'd been pretty stupid about it, assuming the small-town residents wouldn't remember everything they'd said and repeat it to everyone they met. One goon telling the druggist that Angel was his daughter, the other one that she was his niece. Had to get around, and thankfully had to get back to Dan.

She glanced up at him, her eyes shuttered. "Are you going back to town soon?"

He nodded. "Couple of days."

A smile tugged at her mouth. The gesture had his gut tightening. What a sap, reacting like that to a woman's smile...

A couple of days meant respite from guessing games and intrigue. Until he knew the reason for those plates tracing back to the governor, he pretty much had to sit on his hands. Yet, a couple days also meant close and comfortable with this woman.

"I made a pasta casserole with cream of mushroom soup," she announced proudly.

He couldn't help but grin. "Smells incredible."

Leaning in, she whispered conspiratorially, "And nothing's burnt."

In spite of himself, he chuckled. She was just too damn cute. Adorable. That was the word he'd used.

Fit her just right, too. Man, if he didn't watch himself, he could get real used to this scene, to her.

"And for dessert…" She gestured toward the window ledge like a game-show hostess.

Dan walked over, gazed down at one awesome-looking pie. Golden crust, cherry filling oozing out the lattice.

"You made this?" He turned to look at her.

She nodded, beaming.

"It looks amazing, Angel. You must've worked—"

"All day yesterday and today. It took three tries, but I think in this case, the fourth time will be the charm."

Admiration shot through him at rocket speed. Never in his sorry life had he known anyone like her. Determined, intelligent, passionate, down-to-earth, playful. Most of the women he'd gone out with were all about rules and half-truths and diamond-earrings-are-just-not-enough.

No matter what he'd thought before about where she'd come from, this woman was real and genuine and had worked two days to make him dinner.

Talk about humbling. "You are one determined woman."

She smiled shyly, but her smoldering gaze was direct. "Yes I am."

Need shot through him swift and violent. But he held himself in check, remained cool. Although, he wasn't sure how long he could stand the ache.

A smile playing about her lips, Angel went into the kitchen and grabbed a fork out of the drawer. "I think you can do anything if you put your mind to it."

"I agree."

"And if you want something bad enough," she added as she walked toward him.

Her words drifted over his skin like silk. He felt tense, ready to spring, but he held his ground.

She tucked a curl behind her ear, her gaze catlike. "Would you like to taste the pie?"

His pulse kicked. "You offering me a sample, Angel?"

She grazed the pie with the tongs of the fork so the metal prongs were lightly coated with just a little bit of cherry and crust. Not enough to please, but enough to tempt.

His eyes remained on hers as he leaned in, let his mouth close around the metal, saw the pulse at the base of her throat pound a brutal rhythm as he pulled back. "Delicious. I wish I had a prize, maybe one of those blue ribbons, to give you."

She touched his face, smiled softly. "I'd take a kiss instead."

He groaned. "What, are you kidding? That'd be a prize for me."

Real slowly, Angel drew her lower lip between her teeth. For just a moment. She probably didn't even know she was doing it. But the gesture had his mind tripped up and his mouth closing in.

He drew her into his arms and pulled her close. Without thought, he covered her mouth with his. She whimpered, and he shifted, changing the angle of his kiss, playing, tugging, following her as she followed him into one drugging kiss after another.

She pulled back just an inch or so, her eyes fixated on his mouth, her breathing labored.

"You okay?" he asked, not all that sure about himself at the moment.

She nodded, then uttered hoarsely, "I'm sure you're as hungry as I am."

"Angel...you have no idea."

The woman before him took a deep breath, her lips pink and full from his kiss. "Why don't you get washed up for dinner."

"Can I help?"

Angel smiled as Dan walked through the front door, brushing a fleck of Rancon's hay off his shirt. Could he help? Hmm... Now, *that* was a question. Especially when her body hadn't stopped humming all through dinner.

Yes, he could help. He could put her out of her misery, silence that hum.

"You've had a long day," she said, washing the last of the dinner dishes. "Why don't you relax now."

"I'll relax when you relax. What can I do?"

This time she almost told him. "You can dry if you want."

He moved behind her, his warm breath tickling the back of her neck. "Dinner was great. And that pie..."

"Good?"

"Killer."

She glanced over her shoulder. "Surprised?"

"You continually surprise me."

"Is that a good thing?"

"Very good." His arms went around her waist, his hands dipped into the hot, soapy water and found hers.

Heat swirled in her belly as he intertwined his fingers with hers, squeezed. "I thought you were going to dry?"

"I've always been better with water sports." He guided her hand to the sponge, together they clutched it, worked the rough edge against the plate.

As they labored, Dan found her neck with his mouth, giving her restless kisses, grazing his teeth lightly over her skin.

She sucked in a breath. "I like doing the dishes this way."

"I like you." He moved to her ear, whispered, "I'm tired of pretending that I don't need you. I'm through making excuses and backing off when things get too hot and heavy. Tell me you want me, Angel. Tell me it's all right to touch you."

"It's all right. It's all right." Breathlessly, she stood there on shaky legs, her mind a jumble. There was so much more to say. Did she tell him? Right now? Did she tell him that she loved him, that no man had ever touched her like this? Heart or flesh?

But before she could utter a word, his hands were on her belly, wet heat pressing through to her skin. All thoughts were lost as he grazed up her torso, tugging the fabric with him, suds sliding down her belly in his wake.

Her breathing went ragged as he found her, cupping her breasts through the thin fabric of her bra, making her nipples tighten and push through his fingers.

"Dan, I want to..." she started, wanting to say the words, needing for him to know what he'd awakened in her.

He moved closer, his arousal pressing into the small of her back. "Tell me, Angel. Tell me what you want."

She struggled to find her voice as he dragged her bra up, then filled his hands with her once again, taking her nipples between his wet fingers, tugging gently. "Do you like this?"

"Yes." The word came out on a whimper. She let her head drop back against his shoulder, her damp hands fall to her sides.

Dan angled his head to face her, took her mouth under his and tasted as he continued to pinch and flick the hardened peaks.

Something was happening, deep in her belly, a desperate throbbing so foreign it almost frightened her.

And then, as though he knew she ached, knew just where she ached, he let his hand slide, down, down her belly, dipping inside her soft cotton underwear, searching for a spot that even she wasn't familiar with.

"Nice boxers," he murmured.

"They're yours."

"I know."

"I didn't think you'd mind."

"I don't." When he palmed her, found her damp and burning, he released a ragged sound from low in his throat. With his lips hovering above hers, he whispered, "I want to be inside you."

Instinct drove her forward. Hunger drove her forward. Reckless or not, she didn't care. She put her hand over his on the outside of her boxer shorts, and pressed his fingers closer until she felt him hover at the entrance to her body. "Here?"

A single, raw curse tumbled from his lips. "Yes, right here. Where it's wet and hot and—" he slipped a finger inside her "—so tight."

Her breath caught.

His gaze darkened as he looked down into her eyes. "Do you want this?"

"I want you."

"Are you sure?"

"Yes."

"Then come with me."

His hands slipped from breast and core and scooped under her legs, lifting her up. He practically flew into the bedroom, but once there, he laid her on the mattress with great care.

Under the brilliant white moonlight streaming into the room, she watched as he went to the black leather bag that sat on top of a chest of drawers, dived into the side pocket and came up with a foil packet.

Trembling and drenched with need, Angel watched him cross to the bed, stared up into his eyes—they were the eyes of a desperate man. "What's wrong?"

"I really tried to stop this."

"I know."

"For so many reasons I tried to stop this. You're totally vulnerable here. You don't know who you are, where you come from, what you wanted before you walked into this cabin.''

''You're right.'' She stripped off her tank top, unhooked her bra and tossed it to the floor. ''But I know what I want now.''

She was naked from the waist up, but his gaze never flickered from her eyes. ''Is that enough, Angel?''

''More than enough.'' Embarrassment or self-consciousness had no place here, tonight, in this room. She hooked her thumb in the waistband of her boxers. ''I need your help.''

Neither one of them missed the double meaning in those words. Neither one of them could deny wants and needs so strong they had a life of their own. To try would leave them both on the verge of insanity.

His eyes smoldering with desire, Dan deftly removed her panties and his own clothes, all in fewer than five seconds. Then he stood at the foot of the bed, looked down at her. ''You're so dangerously beautiful, Angel.''

Her gaze moved over him possessively. Those handsome, rugged features, muscled torso, washboard abdomen and, her gaze fell…she blushed. ''So are you.''

He grinned like the devil.

She opened her arms. ''Come here.''

The mattress dipped with his weight. Quivering, she waited as he moved over her, wondered as he lowered his head, then sighed as he nuzzled her breast. He made soft circles, until he finally found the center, the tip.

Her cry echoed through the moonlit room as he took her into his mouth, as he suckled and tortured and nipped. The sensation was so shockingly wonderful she near wriggled off the bed.

But Dan held on to her.

With her mind a rainbow of color, she whimpered, her hands searching for him. And she found him. Thick and hot, she held him in her hand.

Jaw clenched, forehead glistening with sweat, his gaze flickered to hers, held. And as they watched each other, he grew harder in her hand.

"No more," he growled, sheathing himself.

"Much more." Angel wrapped her legs around his waist and her arms around his neck.

Raw heat burned from his eyes. "Are you ready?"

"I've been ready since the first night I came here."

He kissed her softly on the mouth, then slid into her body. When she gasped, then cried out, he froze.

Angel felt her muscles contract, then a slight burn rippling through her.

Dan cursed, brought his head up, eyes penetrating her soul just as his arousal penetrated her body. "Angel..."

"I've never been with a man."

"You knew this?"

"I suspected."

"Angel."

The anguish in his eyes ripped her apart. "Dan, please don't pull away."

He groaned with need. "I can't pull away. I don't know how, don't want to know how."

"I don't want to know either."

"Did I hurt you?"

"No." She arched her hips to show him that all the pain was gone, felt the delicious throb and sighed. "There's only heat and sensation and need in me now."

The devil flashed in his eyes once again. "I want them all."

He moved slowly within her, easing himself deeper and deeper, watching her for even a hint of pain, listening as she whimpered for more.

But there was no pain, only heart-wrenching pleasure as she swung her hips back and forth, taking him fully, urging him to move faster and put her out of this sweet misery. Her body sang the tune of pure love as her blood pounded and moved and fed.

And she wondered, for just one moment, if such a moment could be saved.

Then suddenly, torrents of electric heat rushed her from all sides. Desperate to dive directly into the center of it, she thrust her hips up, muscles tight, fingers gripping the sheets.

When the scream of orgasm rippled through her body, when Dan followed her over the edge of that endless cliff, her mind opened.

And like a torrential rainstorm, the whole of her memory came flooding back.

Nine

Her name wasn't Angel.

It was Cathy.

Her Royal Highness, Catherine Olivia Ann Thorne, Princess of Llandaron.

Heart hammering in her chest, she lay there holding the man she loved to her body as her past rushed her like a menacing ocean wave.

Like the ocean waves that crashed against the rocks on Llandaron's picturesque coastline.

Oh God. She remembered. All of it.

As Dan rolled to his side, taking her with him, as her body cooled, yet stiffened with anxiety, set pieces converged on her mind. Eyes closed, her still slightly bruised forehead pressed against Dan's, she saw her lovely childhood, her beautiful rooms in the palace, heard the sweet whisper of her mother's voice, saw her father's eyes. Then there were her brothers, Alex and Maxim, so loving and protective. There was her honorary uncle and town vet, Ranen Turk, and her dear surrogate mother, Aunt Fara.

Her pulse tripped awkwardly. She loved them all so much, missed them terribly, yet her desire to return home, see her family, was lacking. Why?

Curiosity filled her as she searched her memory for more answers.

Still connected in the most intimate of ways, her leg draped over his hip, Cathy pulled herself closer to Dan. He wrapped his arm around her waist and held on tightly, as though he knew she needed his strength. Impossible, she realized, but with his thickly muscled arm around her, his strong, steady heart beating against her breast, he made the angst that dwelled inside her lessen somewhat, somehow made it safe to remember.

In the forefront of her mind, she saw her last day at the castle, saw herself at the welcome-home reception for Maxim and Fran.

Fran. The one person who had known her secret. She had to be worried. Cathy had promised her she would call every three days. No wonder there were people looking for her.

Her heart sank like a stone. Her nightmare. The men following her were her bodyguards. Sent to find her and bring her back. Back to a life consumed in duty. A life that was no life at all.

"Are you okay, Angel?"

Her insides melted like butter at the name, and at

the dangerous and delectable man who uttered it. "Yes."

He nuzzled her neck, flicked his tongue on the spot where her pulse knocked about. A shudder of heat ran through her, followed by the sinking sensation of guilt. She knew what she had to do, should do, right now. Not moan and press her hips to him as she wanted to, but look him in the face and tell him who she was, and who he was protecting her from.

But when he kissed her lips, when her lids rose and her gaze found his, she lost her nerve.

Dangerous Dan Mason was a man of the law. He'd brought her back to the cabin for one reason: to keep her safe while he found out who she was and who was after her. Once he knew she had her memory back, once he knew she was royalty and in absolutely no danger, he would send her packing.

Her spirits twisted and sank. He would send her back to a life that made her desperately unhappy.

She asked herself when she'd run from Llandaron, was peace all she'd been yearning for? Or was she looking to embrace a life with choices as well?

In a mere two days, Dan would return to town and find out everything on his own. Why did she need to speed things along, lose him faster than she had to? Why couldn't she make the choice to follow her heart and embrace these two days?

Her sense of honor tugged, ripped a hole in those queries, then tossed back one of its own; what about Dan's choice?

Heart squeezing with pain, she did the only fair thing, the only right thing. "Dan, there's something I—"

"You're not all right." He caressed her cheek with the back of his hand.

She melted into his touch, begged God to allow her to get lost there.

"Angel? What's wrong?"

Just keep calling me that, she begged him silently. Perhaps it will help me to forget who I really am. "Nothing's wrong."

"Are you sure?"

She nodded. "I'm fine. It's just—"

"Fine?" With a quick grin, he left her for a moment, put on another condom, then dropped into bed and pulled her on top of him. His eyes darkened to coffee-brown as he said playfully, "We can't have fine."

She smiled halfheartedly. He'd misinterpreted her reserved manner. "I didn't mean... Oh, Dan, it was more than fine, way more. It was amazing, out of this world. I never thought I could feel that way."

He brought her head down to him, brushed a kiss on her mouth. "There's so much more, Angel."

Her eyes closed momentarily, mentally putting her hands together, praying that he was right.

He studied her. "You have something on your mind."

"Yes."

"Tell me."

The words were there, so was the truth, resting like a little angel of malice on the tip of her tongue, waiting. She bit her lip. "I want...I want to..." Her words trailed off because she allowed them to, because she was a coward.

He flashed her a smile. "Don't be embarrassed, Angel. I want you again, too." He lifted her up, eased her down on his erection. "All night, all day."

She felt him, inside her, growing harder, thicker. She found his gaze. Again, she tried. "Dan, I really need to…"

But it was too late. The words fell away as his hands slid up her thighs, gripped her hips, rocked her forward gently. "Does this hurt?"

She gasped, her muscles tightening around him. "No."

"Then let me give you what you need, Angel."

As the moon cascaded through the window and the scent of their lovemaking hovered in the air, she watched her lover's eyes turn the color of hot chocolate as he guided her back and forth. "Dan…" But what it was she was begging for, she wasn't certain.

"Take what you want, sweetheart."

She gave up, gave in, took his hands from her hips and thrust them against her breasts.

Tomorrow. She'd tell him tomorrow.

Then she began to move, rocking, bucking, swinging her hips as she felt him strike that spot, that sweet chord within her once again. His muscles flexed under her palms as she squeezed, hearing the whisper of orgasm in her ears.

And as he flicked her nipples between his fingers, told her how beautiful she was, she released the cry of passionate self-indulgence that hovered in her dry throat and rode him into earthshaking climax.

* * *

If he'd done the wrong thing by her, then the devil could take him.

Sunlight moved into the room like a lurking suspect, hanging out, unable to leave the scene of the crime until the Feds, the afternoon shade, came calling.

Angel slept beside him, her tawny curls kissing her creamy shoulders and soft back, looking like the lush angel she was. Snuggled into the crook of his arm, she had one shapely leg draped over his splayed thighs in a dreamy show of possessiveness.

A shot of fire rippled through him, but he willed it to cool. One look, one taste, one touch from her and he knew he'd be done for. How had that happened? he wondered, pulling her closer. How had she made him feel again?

Maybe because she'd given him so much. Maybe because she'd given him herself.

Last night, she'd offered him her virginity. In the bright light of day, he should've felt like a heel for taking what he had no right to want. But he didn't. He felt honored that she'd given him such a precious gift.

Honored, and ravenous for more.

But the time to quell that hunger was limited. He was returning to town to hear her story. And once her identity was revealed, once he'd made sure she was protected, they'd have to go their separate ways. Anyone could tell they were from different and very impenetrable worlds. She was very much alive, while he, well…the jury was still out. And until they cast their verdict, he couldn't allow himself to want or need more than the physical.

Besides, he didn't deserve a woman like her. If he had any sense, he'd get up, get dressed and head back into town right now, see if Jack had anything to report yet.

Beside him, Angel sighed, stretched, her leg inching upward, brushing his arousal.

Dan groaned. The report could wait.

Her lips found his ear, nuzzled, whispered, "Are you awake?"

"Painfully awake."

She licked the curve of his ear. "I know how to put you out of your misery."

"My gun's in the drawer," he muttered, raw heat gripping him.

"No, Deputy, that's not at all what I have in mind." Her husky laughter in his ear had him hard and desperate as hell.

"What's on your mind, Angel?"

Her small hand moved down his chest, his belly tightened when her nails raked over his skin. He dragged in a breath when she found him, held him, stroked him, her lips teasing his neck with butterfly kisses.

Between clenched teeth, he uttered, "You have a wicked touch for an angel."

Her heavenly strokes vacillated from easy to bone-weakening. Her voice remained a husky tease. "I'm guessing you're not used to being on your back, Deputy?"

His hands fisted the sheets.

Her movement quickened, her strokes turning feverish. "And I'm guessing you're also not used to being totally out of control."

She saw too much, way too much. "No, I'm not."

And with that, he had her on her back in seconds. "Any objections, Angel?"

A soft, tender smile playing about her lips, she opened for him. "None."

With a tight jaw and unsteady fingers, he ripped open a foil packet and sheathed himself.

Control was all he had left.

It was the last thought he allowed himself before he buried himself inside her.

"I had no idea that you were a romantic, Dan Mason."

"I'm not."

"Then how do you explain a picnic by the river?"

"It's just lunch."

Cathy laughed at him, knowing that with her, his surly disposition was merely pretense. After all, he'd brought her here, to this beautiful and highly romantic spot. Kind of like a date. He enjoyed the sparring, getting her goat, so to speak. Just as she enjoyed retaliating with a snappy comeback or a probing question.

"You can't fool me, Deputy. You may be a big, bad, tough man of the law, but I know all about that soft side you have hidden."

His gaze moved over her, fairly ate her up. "And I know all about yours."

She grinned. "You're such a smooth talker."

The corners of his eyes crinkled. "And you're just plain smooth. Especially that spot between your—"

"Toes?"

His eyes flashed with amusement. "Sure. There's your toes and your breasts, your lips, your cheeks. But I was actually talking about that delicious and incredibly soft curve between your th—"

"Stop, stop," she cried, releasing a peal of laughter, not meaning her reprimand one bit.

Surely there was nothing like a little sexual tête-à-tête surrounded by aspen and pine under a Wedgwood sky. Especially when the sexiest man alive was doing the tête.

Twenty minutes ago, Cathy had brushed off the urge to spill her guts about her newly found memory, and accepted Dan's proposal for lunch by the river.

And she couldn't think of a better location. For lunch, for romance. Only minutes from the cabin, the spot boasted a curve of grassy hill, plenty of sunny shade and the melodic sounds of birds overhead and water lapping against rock.

Dan popped a handful of raisins in his mouth. "You know, I have to say, I really liked being called, big, bad and tough."

"What about dangerous?"

"Even better."

"I imagine you are dangerous." She sat back against a thick aspen, gnarled with black knots in the shape of a woman's eye. "Do you like being a U.S. marshal?"

"Some days more than others."

"And you catch criminals, right?"

"Fugitives," he corrected, then shrugged. "But, I guess that would make them criminals, too."

She had no idea what made her ask the next question. All she knew was that she couldn't stop the words from spilling out of her mouth. "Have you ever killed anyone?"

His eyes flew up to study her face with a critical squint. "Why do you ask that?"

"I thought that's what we're doing. Asking questions, getting to know each other."

He pitched the raisins back into the bowl. "Well, it's not a very fair playing field, is it?"

"What do you mean?"

"You can't tell me anything about your past, but I'm expected to share mine."

Guilt seeped into her blood like a vicious snake. If she had any pluck, she'd tell him right now, put a thorn right into the side of this wonderful day. But she had no pluck, only love and wishes.

"You don't have to share anything you don't want to share, Dan." Not exactly how she felt, but at least it was fair.

He released a breath through his teeth, dropped back on the blanket, hands behind his head. "I've never killed anyone, all right?" Then he muttered, "Not directly, anyway."

But she'd heard him. Loud and clear. "Not directly?"

"That's right."

"What in the world does that mean?"

"It's nothing. No laws were broken. Nothing."

Curiosity threatened to choke her, but she kept her

mouth shut. She could see by the look on his face, by the set of his jaw, that he wasn't elaborating.

Well, what did it really matter? She didn't care what he'd done in the past. They didn't have to give away snippets of a life that mattered little in the scheme of things. She wouldn't press him and he wouldn't press her.

To lift the mood, she resorted to a woman's cure. "Are you still hungry?"

"Not for raisins."

"How about a sandwich then?"

"Yeah, okay."

"Have half of mine."

He sat up on his elbows, took the sandwich from her and tore into it. It was devoured in about five seconds.

A grin tugged at her mouth. "I think you should have the other half, too."

The wall slipped down again.

"Thanks."

"My pleasure."

"Well, that's all I want, you know." Playfulness and heat returned to his eyes. "Your pleasure."

She grinned shyly. "Eat your sandwich, Deputy."

"Yes, ma'am." He gave her a smile. "And by the way, just for clarification, this isn't just a sandwich. This is a BLT. Love them. Had them all the time as a kid."

"It's the bacon. It's good with anything."

He chuckled. "You're right about that."

"Personally, I loved peanut butter and honey.

Couldn't get enough of it. My brother—'' She stopped short as she realized what she'd just said.

Dan stared at her. "Where did that come from?"

"It just came out," she managed to say, her heart in her throat.

"You have a brother."

"Yes. I guess so."

"Do you remember anything else?"

For a moment she felt as though she were floating, her heart separate from her mind. Did she remember anything else? What a question. Her next sentence would either be the truth or a lie. Her next sentence would decide her immediate future with the man she loved.

Her heart thumped erratically in her chest as she looked Dan in the eye and said, "No, I don't remember anything more."

Something passed over Dan's face. Perhaps she was just imagining things, but she swore he looked relieved.

Cathy picked up a bottle of water and took a healthy swallow. "It's really hot today," she remarked, inching back into the shade of the tree.

"You can take off your top, no one's around."

She tried to look shocked, though inside she was so thankful that he'd brought them back to the comfort and coziness of the tête-à-tête. "What about the animals?"

"If they can go bare, so can you."

"What about you?"

He grinned. "I have no problem getting naked around woodland creatures."

"No." She laughed. "I mean, what about you seeing me?"

"I'm completely for it."

She laughed again, felt a pull deep inside her. "Do you think that a striptease is included in this lunch, Deputy?"

"No, not in the lunch. Maybe in the dessert?"

"But I brought lemon cookies."

He sat up, grinned. "I want skin."

A rush of pink stained her cheeks. Her past contained no wild, impetuous moments like this. Only even keels of loneliness and unfulfilled desires. Until Dan, she'd never undressed for a man, never felt compelled to bare her soul or skin for a man.

But with him, for him, she was a different woman. She was his Angel.

She stood, inched her shirt up over her head. "Were you interested in something like this for dessert?"

His gaze rested on her bare breasts as his hands formed fists in the blanket. "Creamy, sweet, highly edible."

She quivered, her nipples tightening under his gaze.

"But there's only one way to find out, Angel."

She glanced toward the river. "Water looks cool."

"What are you thinking?"

She gave him a coy smile. "A wade in the water?"

"Didn't anyone ever warn you about swimming after eating?"

"If I had someone there to protect me…"

He came to his feet, stood inches from her, his shirt

brushing her beaded nipples. "I'd have to get real close."

"Skin to skin?"

"Exactly." He pulled down her boxer shorts, the ones she was growing so accustomed to wearing.

The summer breeze caressed her hot skin, made her want to fall into his arms. But there was so much to be done first.

Swiftly, she worked the buttons on his shirt, ripping them off when she became frustrated. A few tugs and she had his jeans pooled at his feet, a few seconds and she and Dan were at the water's edge.

The shallow stretch of river ebbed and flowed against their calves. And as they lowered into the cool spring, as Dan eased her back against a slippery rock, let her hips float above the surface, the swirling water acted like a drug.

She wanted him inside her, but he had other ideas.

"Spread your legs for me, Angel."

Anticipation filled her as she followed his command. As the river rushed over her and patches of warm sun beat against her skin, Dan held her hips in his hands, lowered his head and kissed the curls at the juncture of her thighs. "You are so beautiful."

Then he eased her open with his tongue and used his mouth on her.

Cathy gasped, head dropping back as small whimpers of need echoed through the forest, down the riverbank and up, up into the mountains.

"Look at how beautiful you are."

"Dan…"

"Look, Angel."

She lifted her head, opened her eyes. The erotic vision before her had her weak and desperately aroused. Dan's nude body submerged in the water, his dark head lost between her thighs, his tongue easing her apart, searching for the pouty flesh beneath. And when he found it, she cried out, her muscles contracting.

The pressure of his mouth, the raspy flick of his tongue, then the flood of need as he slid his tongue back and inside.

Her head dropped back once again, the water rushed her burning skin.

He held her hips tightly, taking her to the brink, lapping at the pulse of her until she stiffened, screamed her release, for only the woods and mountains and the love of her life to hear.

Ten

Dan woke with a start, disentangled himself from a beautiful sleeping Angel and reached for his gun.

Last thing he wanted to do was leave her, warm and soft and naked. But he'd heard something moving around outside. No doubt it was an animal, but he wasn't taking any chances.

He slipped out of bed, didn't bother with a shirt, just threw on his jeans. He heard the kitchen clock ticking away as he passed through the living room and gave it a quick glance: 10:00 p.m.

He ventured a quick look back at his sleeping beauty, all cuddled beneath the sheets. Time flew when they were together. Hours seemed like seconds. Yet, those seconds were never enough.

Dan turned, headed for the door, wondering if it would ever be enough.

Cool, pine-scented air met him as he stalked outside, gun drawn, eyes peeled, head cocked, listening for a crackle of a branch, rustle of leaves, maybe a couple of greasy foreign accents.

His muscles were springy, alert, his mind quick. As he stared out into the dark night, he silently swore to himself that if anyone came within ten feet of this cabin, he'd take them out. No problem.

But there was no one standing in the small front yard, just groves of moonlit pine, dirt pathways, the tree stump he used to chop wood. He heard the incessant click of crickets in flight, the soft whinny of his horse in the barn and leaves being swatted about by a restless wind.

And yet, he didn't lower his weapon.

If it was just him, if he was alone up here, heard a noise, he'd walk out into the blackness, track the sound, take care of business.

But he wasn't alone up here. He wasn't leaving the porch.

He wasn't leaving Angel.

This violent need that ran through his veins, this need to shield her from all harm, concerned him. Granted, he was a protector by nature, by profession. The instinct had been there from the get-go. But since she'd dropped into his life, looked into his eyes and made his gut coil tighter than a spring, that level of protective instinct had shot off the charts.

At first, he'd been convinced that his need to protect her was just his way of making up for the past, an attempt to fix something that could never really be fixed. Now he wasn't so sure.

He had some serious feelings for the woman in his bed, the tender kind that a man doesn't talk about. Especially when the woman wasn't going to be around for very much longer.

Ice, brittle and sharp, pierced the cage around his heart. *Get used to it, buddy.*

But even though he'd let her go when this was all said and done, he was going to make damn sure he let her go alive.

"Dan?"

His hand tightened around the gun. Every time she'd walked up behind him in that unobtrusive way of hers, he'd heard her, sensed her.

But not tonight.

He was slipping.

Not good.

He turned sharply. She stood on the porch, barefoot, tawny curls tumbling over her shoulders, skin glowing. She was garbed in one of his T-shirts—only the T-shirt. His gaze fell. The blue cotton hit right below that oh-so-sweet spot he'd tasted earlier in the river. So warm in the cool water. His groin constricted.

"Go back inside, Angel."

Her gaze flickered to the Glock in his hand. "What's happening? What are you doing with that?"

"I heard something."

"It's probably just an animal."

"Probably, but I'm not taking any chances." He gestured to the door of the cabin. "Please go back in."

"Not without you."

He sniffed at the slight tip of her chin. "Why are you being so stubborn? I'm trying to keep you safe, here."

"I don't want anyone getting hurt."

His gaze shifted from sexy woman to landscape, then back again. "Even those scumbags who're after you?"

Her face blanched. "You think they could actually find us all the way up here?"

"There's one thing I know. If a man wants something bad enough, he goes to any length to get it."

Their gazes locked for a wisp of a moment, pure sensuality moving from her eyes straight into his heart. How had it happened? he wondered, his forehead creasing into a frown. How had he become a man caught between two needs: the one to possess and the one to protect?

With no clear way out in sight.

"I doubt they're around here," he told her. "But like I said, I'm not taking any chances."

"You realize, we don't even know why they're after me, Dan."

Gun still pointed toward the woods, Dan stared at Angel, his eyes narrowed. "What do you mean by that?"

"Nothing. I'm just being cautious, that's all."

"And calm."

"What?"

"Why are you so calm? You were nervous as hell when you first heard these guys were looking for you." He cocked his head, got a better view of her eyes. "What am I missing?"

The unwelcome tension that had sprouted between them eased suddenly when her gaze raked boldly over him and she said, "All you're missing, Marshal, is being under the covers with me."

Dan shook his head at the rush of wariness and lowered his weapon, feeling the roar of need surge into his blood. Maybe he was getting too hyped up here. Maybe he was seeing and sensing and hearing things that amounted to nothing out of the ordinary.

"And as for being calm," she continued, her gaze playfully seductive, her mouth curving into a smile. "After the afternoon we just had…"

He grinned. "Right."

With an earnest expression, she added, "The truth is, with you, I feel like no one and nothing can enter this perfect little world."

"Angel…" He sighed. *Perfect world.*

He wanted to tell her that no world was perfect. Far from it. He wanted to remind her that she had no past, an uncertain future, two jokers on her ass and a shell of a man who couldn't decide between feeling and running.

But right now, looking into those need-filled amethyst eyes, conversation was the last thing on his mind.

She held out a hand to him. "Put down the gun and come back to bed. I miss you."

As he knew they would, her words oozed over him like honey, sweet and soft. Gun hovering at his side, he started toward her, ready to pull her against him and taste those parted lips.

But he hardly took a step. Behind him, sticks crackled and something shifted in the tall grass. Dan whirled, gun drawn, finger poised on the trigger, roared, "Don't move!"

Angel gasped weakly.

Dan watched as a family of rabbits hopped by, took one look at them and raced for cover, into the safety of the forest.

Dan cursed, reached behind him and shoved his gun in the waistband of his jeans. "I'm going nuts."

"No." He felt her warmth before he felt her arms wrap around his neck. "You're not nuts. You're a wonderful protector."

"I almost wiped out a family of rabbits, Angel."

"But you didn't. You wouldn't have, I know it."

Turning, he gathered her around the waist, pulled her close. She was still a foot or so above him on the porch, and he let his head fall against her chest. Not that he'd ever admit it out loud, but for some reason she made him feel safe, too. Go figure.

He felt her shiver. "You're cold."

"I'm fine."

"Not fine again."

She laughed softly. "Well, there is a way and a place to warm me up again."

He glanced up at her. "Yeah? Where's that?"

Her laughter eased into a flirtatious curve of the lips as she reached around behind her back, seized his hands and slid them down to cup her backside. "If you're really in need of someone to capture…"

His body shot to attention and his mind refused to call up anything but her. This was the thing his boss had always warned him about. Getting too close to a case.

And Angel was his case, had to be.

"Take me to bed, Dan."

Someday soon, reality would swoop in and swallow them both whole. But not tonight. Not tonight.

"That's Deputy U.S. marshal to you, Ma'am." He ducked his head, eased her onto his shoulder, then lifted and whisked her inside, leaving only the teasing sound of her laughter to the stars, sky and cool mountain air.

"Poor Rancon, two people riding on him."

Dan stifled a laugh. "Trust me, Angel, after all that time cooped up in his stall, he's dying for the exercise. Besides, it's good for his leg."

As if agreeing with his master, the black stallion gave a regal snort and picked up his already brisk pace down the thin mountain trail.

"Hold me tighter, Angel."

Arms wrapped around Dan's waist, Cathy shifted in the makeshift blanket saddle, then pressed her breasts against his back and squeezed. "Yes, sir."

"Sir? I like that." Even over the *clip-clop* of Rancon's hooves against the packed-dirt trail, she could fairly hear Dan grin.

"Then I won't say it again," she joked.

"Why not?"

"You're far too full of yourself already."

He glanced over his shoulder, tossed her a fiery look. "I'd much rather be full of you."

Happiness and heat filled her. It was the delightful

combination that swam in her blood every time he looked at her with that steady, smoldering gaze. "We can go back to the cabin," she suggested.

"Not yet." As Rancon's body shifted between her legs, Dan shot her a dangerous grin full of promises, then turned back to face the trail. "Be patient, Angel. First one ride, then the other."

Cathy feigned shock. "What a thing to say."

"I got plenty more where that came from."

"I'm sure you do. Who taught you such vulgarity?"

"The boys down at the office. They're a bad influence on me. You know, impure thoughts on a pure mind and all that."

"Shameful." Pure mind, indeed. She grinned, held back laughter.

"They're not all bad guys, though."

"No?"

"They clean it up around their wives and kids."

"Good to know."

For a moment, the only sounds were nature's and, of course, Rancon. She loved to ride, had for most of her life. But with Dan, riding was an altogether different experience.

Above, clouds moved across the sun, sending cool air their way. So the unstable atmosphere was ripe for Dan's query. "Do you think you have any kids, Angel? Obviously not biological, but maybe adopted?"

Her heart dipped as Rancon loped over a fallen tree. Once, because she'd always dreamed of having a brood of children. But with no husband or even the slight possibility of one...well, she'd had to put that dream on the back burner. And twice for a new reason altogether. She saw, in her mind's eye, a child with the violet eyes of her mother and the stubborn chin and splendid courage of her father.

"No, I don't think I have any children. Do you think you have a wife?"

He fairly scoffed. "No."

She laughed. "You're not really the marrying kind, are you?"

"Never thought so. But I was engaged once upon a time."

A soft gasp escaped her, surprised again by this unpredictable man. "You were?"

"Yep."

"How long ago?"

"Four years."

She heard the tightness in his tone, but didn't ask the flock of questions that balanced precariously on the tip of her tongue. The answers, she decided, might be too painful to hear, might make her incredibly jealous or worst of all, endear her to him further.

The route she took wasn't altogether emotion-free, but it was the lesser of two evils. "Did you want children? Do you want children?"

"I love kids. They're great," Dan said evasively.

"You just executed a better side step than Rancon."

He released a weighty sigh. "The way I grew up...it was hardly the perfect role model for good parenting skills."

"I imagine no household is perfect." Above them, several more clouds moved in, their puffy whiteness taken over by ribbons of gray, blocking the sun's warmth.

"No kid deserves someone like me."

"Dan, that's ridic—"

"Seriously, Angel. I hunt down bandits for a living, carry a semiautomatic weapon and travel four days out of seven."

"That sounds like your job, not you."

"They're one and the same. I'm not looking to be tied down and civilized."

An unruly wind picked up then, sending the first sprinkles of a potential rainstorm through the air. "Because of what happened four years ago?"

"Because of who I am now."

"And who are you, Dan?"

"I'm a recluse and a pain in the ass." He groaned. "Dammit, Angel. You know I hate these probing questions. Especially when you have nothing to offer in return."

She didn't shrink at his frustration, only at the reminder of all that she was withholding from him. Trained to deal with people in emotional states, and highly charged, sometimes politically dangerous situations, she instinctively aimed for peace.

"All right, Dan."

"All right? Just like that? No argument?"

"No argument. I'm not going to push you for answers you're not comfortable giving. If you want to share something with me in the future, you'll have to bring it up yourself."

She'd stunned him into silence, she quickly realized when he blithely remarked, "I swear to God, I've never met anyone like you, Angel."

"Is that a compliment?"

"Yes."

"Thank you."

"I'm thinking you must be some kind of diplomat." He glanced over his shoulder, eyebrow raised. "What do you think?"

She managed a tremulous smile. "Anything's possible."

Sprinkles quickly turned to droplets. The sun had all but disappeared.

"Weather's turning," Dan remarked, shielding his face from the rain as he looked up. "Dark clouds. Could have some lightning."

"Rancon's getting soaked."

Dan turned the horse around, headed back in the direction of the cabin. "So are we."

"I know, but I feel badly for him."

"It'll cool him off a little."

"Us, too?" She smiled to herself.

"Around you, Angel, my blood is always boiling."

"Another compliment?"

Pulling up the reins, he brought Rancon to a halt, then turned his upper body to face her. "Definitely."

As the wind tossed sheets of rain back and forth like a fierce game of tennis, Dan leaned toward her, brushed a butterfly kiss over her mouth. "You and the rain…what a combination."

"Like champagne and caviar," she whispered against his mouth.

"Like bust and convict."

With a grin, he brushed another soft kiss on her mouth. Cathy sighed, waiting for more, wanting more, her mouth burning with liquid fire. Then his hand went to her neck, drawing her closer, and she felt lost, to the elements, to him, as Dan plied her with a series of hungry kisses. When she boldly laved his upper lip, he invaded her mouth with his tongue, twining with hers in a heady game of desire.

Trying to show him her heart, Cathy returned his bone-melting kisses with every ounce of love she felt. Sharp pangs of need and want flooded her belly as the rain flooded them, running down their noses, into their open mouths.

Dan drew back with a tortured groan. She smiled at him, and he pushed a soaking-wet curl from her cheek. "We should get back."

"And get dry."

He smiled suggestively. "Well, I don't know about that."

"Hot shower?"

"With both of us behind the shower curtain this time?"

She laughed. "Turn around and tell Rancon to giddy up."

Dan eased the stallion into a brisk walk with just a word and they headed for home. Minutes into the journey, Dan called over his shoulder, "I've decided to take Rancon into town tomorrow."

As the rain pummeled her body and face, Dan's announcement pummeled her heart. "So soon?"

"For him or for me?"

She didn't answer him, didn't have to.

''I told you I was going to take care of you, all the way to the end of this mystery.''

She suddenly felt very cold. ''I know you did. And I appreciate it. It's just been so…''

''I know,'' he called back. ''But I told Jack I'd get back to him in a couple days.''

''And it's been a couple days.''

''Yeah, it has.''

She leaned in, close to his ear. ''Do you think he'll have some information?''

''Jack's the best there is. I'm guessing he'll at least know who's following you. Maybe even why. And if he's really on top of things, he may even know who you are.''

As they neared the cabin, Cathy couldn't suppress the shivers that ran through her. She couldn't let him go. She couldn't let him find out the truth.

Behind them, lightning crackled in the sky.

She'd just have to think of some way to keep him in bed tomorrow.

Eleven

"They're called s'mores." Dan impaled a fat white marshmallow with one of the tree branches he'd whittled down to a thin pokerlike tool.

Cathy watched in fascination as he set it over the ginger flames shooting out from the dry wood in the fireplace. "I don't think I've ever had a s'more."

Dan stared at her with mock astonishment. "You must've been pretty deprived as a kid."

"Probably." As she took the stick he'd made for her and placed a marshmallow at the tip, she mentally rolled her eyes. Deprived. If he only knew. A wonderful family and a wonderful home. There were ponies and fine clothes, servants and balls and jewels. Most people's fantasy. Perhaps she'd been selfish to wish for love, too. Perhaps she should be grateful for this time she was granted.

Her gaze moved over the man she loved. Yes, she was grateful. For a few weeks of freedom and for this man who made her knees weak and her heart sing.

"Watch out, Angel."

So caught up in her thoughts, Cathy hadn't been watching what she was doing. When she pulled her stick back from the fire, a flame had enveloped her marshmallow.

Hastily, she blew out the tiny blaze, then turned to Dan and shook her head. "I thought my days of burning food were over."

He chuckled at her dejected expression. "Don't worry. See, in the world of s'mores, a burnt marshmallow is a good thing."

"No it's not. You're just trying to be sweet."

He raised an eyebrow. "I don't do sweet. You know that."

"True," she said, a grin tugging at her mouth.

"Go on and taste it—see for yourself."

If he was playing a joke on her, making her bite into something that tasted like a cinder block or an ash tray, she'd be exacting her revenge immediately. Perhaps more tickling or something equally torturous.

Amusement glowed in his eyes. "Don't be a chicken."

She tipped up her chin. "I am not a chicken."

"Glad to hear it. Now, get to it."

She felt his eyes on her as she wrapped her lips around the marshmallow and pulled back. Sweet, light, crispy… She looked up. "It's delicious!"

"I told you so." His gaze remained on her mouth.

"What's wrong?" she asked.

"Just this," he muttered, leaning in close, until his mouth was a mere whisper from hers. "You've got a little—" his tongue traced the soft fullness of her lower lip "—marshmallow."

Liquid heat surged into her belly, making her hungry, painfully hungry. But he didn't cover her mouth with his, didn't give her what she needed, those slow, shiver-inducing kisses.

No. He pulled back, grinned and whispered, "You're right. Delicious."

"Tease," she muttered dryly.

"First things first, Angel. I promised to show you how to make a s'more."

"You mean, the marshmallow toasting's not all there is to it?"

"What? Are you kidding?"

"Way more advanced, huh?"

"Way." A half smile hovered on Dan's lips.

Pressing down the currents of desire that raged in her blood, she watched him assemble a s'more. First he toasted another marshmallow. "We get a graham cracker, then we put on the chocolate, then comes the marshmallow."

"And I suppose the hot marshmallow melts the chocolate?"

"You are so brilliant."

She laughed at his sincerely impressed expression.

"Did you eat these a lot as a child?" she asked when he handed her the sandwich.

"Whenever we could get our hands on a couple chocolate bars and a lighter."

What different childhoods they'd had. Yet both

lived in a sort of unseen prison. Would he look at her differently if he knew how she'd grown up? *When* he knew, she reminded herself.

"You toasted marshmallows with a cigarette lighter?"

He nodded.

"That sounds very dangerous, Dan."

"How do you think I got this way?"

"Dangerous?"

"Yep."

"Obviously with little supervision."

"Try none. I pretty much grew up in foster care."

"The foster care system in this country has made some wonderful advances in the last few years. I've found—"

She came to a screeching halt, her gaze flickering to his. Dan had that investigatory gleam in his eyes, his lips parted, ready for questions.

She quickly supplied him with an answer. "I must work with children."

It wasn't exactly forthcoming, but it wasn't untrue. In her travels, she worked with and for children all the time, as an advocate, a friend and a fund-raiser.

"Well, that explains it."

"Yes."

"I suppose we'll know for sure tomorrow."

She forced a smile. "I can't wait."

"Really?"

"No, not really."

A glow of pleasure passed over his eyes. He glanced down at her chocolate, marshmallow and graham cracker sandwich. "You gonna eat that or not?"

She gladly followed him into the blissful world of playful repartee, anything to forget that tonight might be the last time they were together, the last time he looked on her as a normal girl. "Are you coveting my s'more, Marshal?"

"Not just the s'more."

"Ah," she smiled, "the both of us."

There was something about him, about this situation that was highly conducive to wild, wanton behavior. She was fairly certain that in Llandaron, around the conservative court, the thought of brushing a melted-chocolaty concoction over her lips, sliding it down her neck and into the valley between her breasts, wouldn't even have entered her mind.

But she wasn't in Llandaron.

She was here. And as she sat beside a roaring fireplace with the sound of the rain beating against the cabin roof, the thoughts came, followed by the action.

"What are you doing, Angel?" His husky tone suggested he knew full well what she was doing, yet couldn't believe what he was seeing.

"You said you wanted both of us."

"I did."

She smiled. "Then come and get us."

Dan thought his mind was about to explode. Into brilliant colors of her. Dressed in a clean pair of his boxers and one of his white tank undershirts, her hair falling around her shoulder, she leaned toward him. She was so close, scented, painted with melted chocolate, her half-lidded eyes dripping with temptation.

His body pulsed with need.

"Start here," she whispered, pressing her lips to his.

The sweetness of chocolate, of her, raged into his

bloodstream. His hand found the base of her neck, jerked her closer. They could linger over each other later, much later. Right now she needed to be devoured—and he needed to take.

He tilted his head, took her mouth at another angle, took pride and pleasure from her moans at the battle of lips and tongue and teeth she fought along with him.

When he ached to taste, he moved down, kissed her jaw, then her neck. She let her head fall back, but threaded her hands in his hair and pressed him closer. He deepened his kiss at the base of her neck where her pulse thrummed, where her skin felt slick and hot.

"More," she uttered on a desperate groan.

She could have whatever she wanted, whenever she wanted it. He moved down, following the path of chocolate she'd set for him with his teeth and tongue. Her breathing turned ragged. Then suddenly, her hands found the border of her tank, pulled the fabric down and bared her breast.

Dan went hard as granite.

He took the small globe in his hand, kneaded, died as she gave soft little whimpers of pleasure, then lowered his head and suckled. A cry escaped her throat, followed by a raw, frantic curse. One he too wished to utter for so many reasons—reasons he didn't want to face or analyze.

So instead, with quick fingers, he stripped her bare, then himself. She murmured, "Yes, yes," over and over as he slid over her body, feeling her damp curls against his thighs, her beaded nipples against his chest. But when she wrapped her legs around him, time stopped.

Dropping down, he found her passion-filled gaze

and pushed slowly into her body. Outside, the rain rapped against the roof and windows in a frenzied rhythm. Dan followed that rhythm, took her, took them both into a world of unknown pleasure.

Higher and higher they climbed as she bucked and he plundered. When the lightning crashed outside the window, so did his Angel. And with his mouth on hers, he followed.

"Angel?"

"Yes."

"You awake?"

"Uh-huh." Wrapped in a blanket, wrapped in Dan's arms, beside the receding fire, Cathy lifted her head from his chest and glanced up at the clock on the kitchen wall: 2:45 a.m. Why did time run on with no care for the people who lived in it?

Threading his hand in her hair, Dan eased her head back to his chest. Strange, but his heartbeat felt suddenly stronger against her cheek. "Should we go to bed?"

"Not yet."

"Is something bothering you?"

He took a moment before answering, his arms tightening around her. "You know when you asked me if I'd killed anyone?"

Her pulse kicked to life, echoing the solid hammering in his chest. "I remember."

He sighed. "My partner was killed four years ago. I was laid up in the hospital with an injury and couldn't be out with her on the job."

Stomach clenching, she said, "Her?"

"Her."

"She wasn't just your partner, was she?"

"No."

The room began to spin.

"She was my fiancée."

Cathy's breath caught in her throat, but she managed a weak, "What happened?"

"We were tracking down a skip. Real bastard. Before I could cuff him, he popped me one, sent me to the hospital. Janice was determined to bring him in. So, she went out with some rookie."

"Oh, Dan…"

"I wasn't there to protect her, Angel."

Cathy didn't say anything, just held on to him. Suddenly, everything that had happened over the past week made sense, his attitude about life, and marriage and people—and his dedication to protect her.

"The guy that took her out got away. I spent four years tracking him, waiting for him to put one foot over the line. Finally I caught a break, snagged him at a friggin' car wash."

"What happened then?"

"After a struggle, I took him in. He's in jail now."

"You hurt him, didn't you?"

"A few bruises."

She sat up. "Dan."

"He had a few stitches."

"You hurt him."

"Damn right I did," he exploded, sitting up, his eyes close to menacing. "He deserved a helluva lot more."

"Is that why you're up here?"

He nodded. "Got suspended. Indefinitely. Supposed to be thinking about what I did. Like I could help thinking about it."

Cathy touched his hand. She felt no judgment, only understanding for a man tormented by the past.

"You loved her?"

"Of course I did."

There were tears in her eyes, imagining what it would be like to lose someone you love. Losing her family. Losing Dan. "I'm so sorry, Dan."

His gaze found hers, something close to love burned there. "You know what, Angel? I pretty much died that day. Never thought I'd feel again. Unless it was like total shi—" He shoved a hand through his hair. "But then…"

"Then what?"

His gaze grew tender. "You."

"Dan—"

"I don't know what that means, Angel. But I do know that you're the one person who's made me feel anything in a long time. You are so amazing, so open, so…real. I was serious when I said that I've never met anyone like you."

Guilt threatened to choke her. She had to tell him the truth. Right now. He'd just laid his past, his heart bare. What was she going to do about it? Be the woman who loved him or be the coward of her past?

"Angel, come here." He eased on a condom and pulled her on top of him, kissed her softly on the mouth as the rain reared back to a light sprinkle and the fire turned to embers.

"Dan, I have something to say."

"No more talking."

"But—"

"Come on, Angel. I just spilled my guts all over the place here. I need you." His eyes implored her.

Pressing against her abdomen was the evidence of that need.

"I need to be inside you, Angel."

Her heart ached just as her body ached. She lifted her hips, felt him at the entrance to her core, and gave in to the hiding place that his desire allowed. She grabbed his hands and placed them on her hips.

And in one sleek movement, he brought her down, took her home.

Cathy felt the warmth and the brilliance of the morning sun against the back of her eyelids. Under the soft sheets, she stretched, her body stiff and sore from a night of lovemaking. A smile tugged at her mouth as she recalled the sprint they'd taken to the bed around three or four that morning. Then there were the strange positions they'd come up with.

On a sigh, she let her leg drift to the right side of the bed, on the lookout for Dan's thickly muscled thigh. But all she encountered was tangled sheets.

Her eyes flew open with a start. She looked around, saw nothing except a clock that read noon.

Fear knotted inside her as she ripped off the covers and slipped on her clothes. She ran all over the small cabin calling for him. But he was gone. She went outside, her gaze searching every inch of land in her sights. Nothing. Her throat went dry as a basket of cotton. How could he just leave without a word? she wondered pitifully. And the stables only held more bad news. Rancon was gone.

Oh, God.

As promised, he'd gone to town. Panic rioted within her. He'd gone to town to hear from someone else's lips that she was a princess and that the men who followed her were her bodyguards.

She dropped to the stoop, put her head in her hands.

How could she have been such a coward? How could she have thought that she could keep him here for another day?

As she was about to let the tears come, the tears that had taken up residence ever since she'd woken up ten minutes before and found him gone, she heard a crackle, a shifting in the trees.

Her heart leaped.

Dan.

He hadn't gone to town. Just for a ride in the woods, maybe went fishing down the river…

But when she stood, put her hand to her forehead to block the sun, her jubilant celebration died. Coming through the woods on two snorting pintos were Peter and Cale, her bodyguards. They rode directly up to her and inclined their heads.

"Your Highness?"

With great effort, she tipped up her chin. "Yes."

"We've come to take you home."

Twelve

Dan shoved his foot into the stirrup and leaped onto Rancon's back. In just over a week, he'd turned into a romantic fool.

He glanced down at the weeds in his hand, shook his head. Picking violets for the woman who lay asleep in his bed. The boys at the field office would have a ball with that piece of news.

But Dan couldn't stop the grin that tweaked his mouth, picturing her delight—and his reward.

With a gentle kick, he set Rancon off back toward the cabin. The day was shaping up to be beautiful. Bright sunshine and not too hot, perfect day to spend by the river or, his grin widened, in the river.

Suddenly that smile faded a touch. He should've been on his way to town, to get that information from Jack. He owed it to Angel to find out who she was, who she belonged to. Truth was, he just didn't want anything interfering with what she liked to call "their little world." At least for one more day.

Romantic fool.

He continued to bawl himself out as he rode through the clearing. But when he got close to the cabin, something in the air shifted. He couldn't make it out, not yet. The sun still shone, the birds still twittered, but he knew that there was something off.

Then he saw it.

Heart in his throat, Dan pulled back hard on the reins, slid off Rancon and reached for his gun.

Standing on the porch, directly in front of Angel, were the two Euro-trash greaseballs from town. Instincts on high, he visually checked for weapons, saw that one of them was holding something dark. Dan couldn't make out what it was, but it had his gut tight as hell.

The men were talking, their expressions rigid. Whatever it was about, he thought, Angel looked upset.

Gun drawn, Dan stalked toward them. When he was about ten feet away, he aimed and shouted menacingly, "Drop it!"

The two men turned, squinted. Then they turned back to Angel and said something.

Anger dripping in his blood, Dan moved closer, his body and senses peaked with tension. "Drop it or I drop you!"

Angel, her eyes wide and fearful, stepped in front of the smaller of the two men. "No, Dan, please—"

"Don't move, Angel," he commanded. He was within five feet of his target now.

The giant to her right sneered. "I suggest you stop right there and put your weapon down, sir."

Dan muttered a raw two-word phrase and kept coming, his arm fully extended.

"Dan, please," Angel begged, her hands reaching toward him. Then she turned to Goon One and said in an imperious tone, "Cale, don't you dare touch him!"

Behind her, the smaller goon said, "But, Your Highness, he has held you hostage."

Dan felt as though he'd been sucker punched in the gut or maybe he'd been boxed in the ears. He hadn't heard the guy correctly. There was no way.

Angel was shaking her head at the smaller man. "No, he helped me, Peter."

"Your Highness, it's common in these situations to think—"

"Your Highness?" Dan's hand tightened on the gun. "What the hell are they talking about, Angel?"

The goon called Cale ignored him, addressed Angel. "The king was certain that you'd been abducted, Your Highness. Is this not the case?"

"The king?" Dan roared before transferring his weapon into his left hand. He'd had enough of this bull. Time for action. In three seconds, he had Cale in a headlock, gun clattering to the ground. "Someone better tell me what's going on here."

Cathy felt sick to her stomach, her head pounding like a jackhammer. How had she allowed this to happen? How had she allowed things to go so far? She'd been unbelievably selfish, that's how.

On shaky legs she walked over to Dan. He stared at her, through her, confused and ready to do battle with anyone and everything. Her throat went tight. Lord, this was not how this should have played out. But she had no choices now, only the horrible job of telling the man she loved the truth about who she was and what she'd done. "Let him go, Dan. Please."

He shook his head, spoke with deathly calm. "Not until I know what this is about."

A warning voice in her head whispered for her to run, run away, but she brushed the feeling aside. Running wasn't always as safe as it seemed. Besides, she was through with acting the coward.

On a thick swallow, she faced him. "My name is Cathy. Catherine Olivia Ann Thorne. Princess of Llandaron."

His mouth dropped an inch, he hissed, "That's crazy, Angel."

"I ran away from home, Dan." She released a pathetic chuckle. "For once in my life I needed to feel freedom. So I came here to the mountains and—"

"Are you telling me that you're…royalty?"

She nodded stiffly, her cheeks flushed with humiliation. "These men are my bodyguards."

Dan cursed, released the man he still held in a choke hold.

"We need to talk, Dan. Please. Can we go into the cabin?"

His eyes narrowed, he scoffed. "I'm not going anywhere."

With as much calm as she could muster, Cathy turned to Cale and Peter. "Please wait for me in the house."

The two men hesitated only a moment before bowing and doing as she commanded.

When the door closed behind them, Cathy took a deep breath and continued, "When you and Rancon startled me, when I fell, I lost my past, totally and completely. I had no idea who I was until..." She paused, knowing that what she had to say next was going to threaten everything they'd shared over the last week. But as Fara always said, "When something pains you, you've got to take your medicine."

"Until?" he drawled dangerously. "Until when, Angel?"

Oh God, could she say it? She had to. She owed him that much. "My memory returned on the night we came back from town."

His eyes turned wide and thunderous. "Are you telling me that you've known who you are for two days?"

She nodded, shame eating away at her soul.

"So, you've been lying to me for two days?" A muscle flicked angrily in his jaw.

"I'm so sorry, Dan."

"Sorry you lied or sorry you got caught?"

"Dan, I swear, I wanted to tell you. I was going to tell you last night, but you wouldn't—"

"Are you about to use me as an excuse?"

She paled. "No. Of course not. You're right. I had

time to tell you and I didn't.'' Her breath caught, so close to tears. ''I didn't want you to leave. I didn't want to leave you.''

A brief shadow of tenderness darkened his eyes, but it quickly retreated in favor of fury. ''Do you actually think I'm going to believe anything you say? How do I know that you haven't been lying to me from the beginning?''

She shook her head. ''I haven't.''

He grabbed her by the shoulders. ''Was this some game to you? Runaway princess looking for a little blue-collar fun?''

''No,'' she said breathlessly. ''God, no.''

His eyes searched hers almost desperately, then he snarled and released her, turned away. ''You must've laughed your ass off whenever I told you how amazing you were, how real and honest you were.''

Tears hovered behind her eyes, but she wouldn't give in to them. ''Listen to me. I didn't tell you because I didn't want our time to end. I fell in love with you, Dan Mason. Head over heels in love. I didn't want to lose you.''

''Well, guess what, sweetheart?'' he snapped. ''You lost me.''

His words fisted around her heart like a vise, creating a pain so brutal she thought she'd never recover. But she continued to fight. ''Dan, look in my eyes.''

He ignored her.

About to lose the most wonderful thing in her life, Cathy raked up every ounce of courage she had, grabbed Dan's shoulder and urged him to face her. ''Look in my eyes, dammit!''

Slowly, his stony gaze rose to meet her.

As the soft summer breeze blew her hair around her face, she said, ''Do you believe that I only found out who I was a few days ago?''

Without hesitation. ''No.''

The vise compressed. ''Do you believe I love you?''

He shot her a cold stare. ''Maybe your question should be, do I even care?''

Tears of shock and pain spilled down her cheeks. She understood his bitter anger. What she'd done had sent him back into fear mode. And like a wild animal that had been hurt again and again, it was clawing at its cage when it felt threatened.

''All right,'' she said, swiping at the tears on her cheeks as she strove for courage. ''I deserve your anger. But you know what you deserve, Dan Mason? A living, breathing woman who loves you and wants to make you happy. A woman who will bring you back to the world of the living.''

The rage slipped a little, but swiftly moved into hostility.

She took a frustrated breath. ''You're only seeing what you want to see here, aren't you, Dan?''

''And what is that?''

''An easy way out.''

Cold eyes sniped at her. ''Maybe you should get going, Your Highness. Back to your country, your kingdom.''

She straightened her spine. ''You're right. I should. I've run long enough and far enough.''

The old gypsy woman's words rippled inside her

heart. Take great care...well she'd taken great care. But she wasn't lost as the woman had warned. No. In fact, a new strength resided in her. From love and from pain. And though the thought of leaving this cabin and the man she loved horrified her, she had to do what she had to do. She was ready to return home and face her father, and a future of her own choosing.

She turned to go into the cabin, collect her things, but paused on the porch. "Running gets awfully tiring."

Dan glanced up. "I've got plenty of energy."

"I'm not going to beg or plead with you to believe me, forgive me or understand why I did what I did. We all have to take our own journey in this life. I was just hoping that we would take ours together."

For one brief moment, Dan seemed to sway toward her, but another second later he was on Rancon's back, riding back into the woods.

Leaving Cathy to whisper into his dust, "Goodbye."

Thirteen

Dan fisted his beer, tipped it back and let fly.

Directly in front of him, the sign for Denver Sheff's Tavern blinked neon red in the dim light, warning him that maybe it was time to stop or at least slow down.

But he signaled for Sheff to bring him another.

Hey, it was only nine o'clock. Too early to go home to an empty apartment. Besides, he never paid attention to warnings. Of any kind.

The note that Angel—correction, that Princess Catherine Thorne of Llandaron—had left for him on the kitchen table before she'd taken off a few days earlier twitched in his wallet. He'd read it a hundred times, and like a total jerk, hadn't been able to toss it out. A measly six words had haunted his days and his nights.

I'm sorry. I love you. Angel.

He swore under his breath, rammed a hand through his hair. Haunted him enough to pack up and leave the cabin right after she had, head back to Denver. The bed, the shower, the kitchen, the fireplace, the river, the scent of pine—everything reminded him of her.

A deep chuckle erupted from behind him. "I'd buy you a beer, Mason, but it looks as though you've had enough."

"I'm not driving." Dan stole a glance over his shoulder, then scowled when he saw Jack Bonner coming his way. "How'd you know I'd be here, Bonner?"

"Sheff's got that extra-dark feeling-sorry-for-yourself beer on tap."

"Get lost."

Jack settled onto the bar stool beside him. "Not a chance, Deputy."

"If you haven't heard, I'm no longer employed with the Deputy U.S. Marshal Service," he grumbled.

"I heard you quit The DUSMS."

"That's right."

"Thrill of the chase is gone, huh?"

"Something like that." Something exactly like that. He'd spent four years looking for revenge. Sure, he'd found some satisfaction. But mostly he'd found emptiness.

That is, until a violet-eyed beauty had stepped into his path.

"You could always come on over to the intelligence side of things. I'm looking for a partner."

"CIA never interested me."

"It's the FBI." Jack grinned. "But that's a good one, man, real funny."

"I try."

"Maybe you could do stand-up."

"Right," Dan snapped back.

Jack's grin widened. "Problem is, you got one helluva protective instinct. Needs to be fed."

Dan stared at him as though he were crazy. "What are talking about?"

"You know exactly what I'm talking about." Jack ordered a beer from the bartender. "Speaking of which, what happened to our princess?"

"She's not 'our' anything," Dan snarled.

Jack burst out laughing. "Wow, you got it bad, buddy."

"Shut your mouth or I'll do it for you."

Sheff set a cold one down in front of Jack. "You boys take it easy now. You know I don't allow fists in here, especially over something as ridiculous as your love lives."

"Who the hell said anything about love?" Dan shot them both subzero glares. "This isn't about love."

Jack winked at the bartender. "Don't worry about it, Sheff. I got him under control."

Sheff raised his eyebrows and muttered, "I hope so."

Dan shook his head, said quietly, "I said *nothing* about love."

Before heading down the bar to another customer, Sheff said, "That one's got it bad."

Jack tossed up his hands in triumph. "Twice in a

matter of minutes. You know what we call that in the bureau, Mason?''

''Two idiots running off at the mouth?'' Dan countered dryly.

''Try a forgone conclusion.''

I'm sorry. I love you. Angel.

How long was it going to take to get her out of his head? How much would he have to drink?

''Why are you here, Bonner?'' Dan grumbled, taking another pull on his beer.

''To stop you from making the biggest mistake of your life.''

''I think you're wasting your time.''

''And I think you should go after her, tell her you love her, ask her to marry you.''

Dan tapped his beer. ''How many of these did you have before you came over here? You don't even believe in marriage.''

''Maybe not for myself. But you got to be put out of your misery, pal.'' He grinned broadly, took a swallow of his beer and said, ''Yeah, I know, that means she's gonna get stuck with your sorry ass. But I don't see any other way.''

''The woman's a princess, Jack. Royalty, for chrissakes.'' Royalty. Dan practically choked on the word.

''So what?''

''So, she's used to furs and diamonds and castles and sh—''

''You have a lot to offer—''

''I have nothing to offer.''

''But you love her, pal.''

''Yeah, but it's not enough.'' Dan went stock-still.

He wanted to drag those words back. But it was too late. He heaved a sigh, his hand tightened around the neck of his beer bottle.

Of all the stupid things to do. Fall in love with a princess.

"Does she love you?"

He shrugged, sighed. "That's what she says. But then again, she also said she couldn't remember anything when she knew exactly who she was."

Jack grimaced. "I know you get why she did that, Mason. And I know you get why you're letting her little trump piss you off so much."

In that moment, Dan hated the fact that Jack knew him and his past so well. Sure, he believed that she'd had memory loss, and that she'd wanted to hold on to the last two days. He believed it because he'd wanted those days, too. He'd have probably done the same thing to stay with her a little longer.

Dan leaned back against the bar stool. "I'm not good enough for her."

"Well, that's true."

A dry chuckle escaped his throat. "You're such an ass."

"I know. So are you, though."

"Yeah."

Jack drained his beer. "So, you're not good enough for her. Who the hell is, right? But I'll tell you one thing, Dan, there's some guy out there who doesn't care if he's good enough or not, he just wants her bad enough to risk it all. He's waiting for her to come home all brokenhearted, waiting to offer her a shoulder to cry on."

"Shut up!" Dan's jaw threatened to crack. He couldn't even imagine that, refused to imagine that.

He stood up, ripped out his wallet and snatched up a crisp twenty, tossed it on the bar. In his haste, the note, her note, escaped and fluttered to the floor.

Before Dan could move, Jack dived for it. But he didn't look inside. Instead, he held it close to the candle on the bar.

He tossed Dan a wry look. "So, pal. What do you want me to do with this?"

"I swear to you, I eat a pound a week and never get sick of it. How do you explain that?"

Cathy smiled at Fran. "You're pregnant."

Fran grimaced. "How do you explain it *before* I was pregnant?"

Cathy laughed, Fran, too, as they stood under the famous Gershin Taffy Shop's new green awning at noon on a very sunny Monday afternoon. Summer was in full swing and the town was swarming with tourists. The veterinary clinic that Fran and Ranen had opened was closed today, and the two women had escaped the warmth of the castle and ventured into the coolness of the seaside town.

It was good to be home, Cathy mused. Good to see her family. Unexpectedly, they provided a great deal of comfort to her right now as she tried desperately to forget her time in the mountains of Colorado.

Ironic. All that time without a memory and now she was wishing for that impediment to return for just a day or so.

No. That wasn't right. She was a different woman

now, no longer living her life in the shadow of her own fears and insecurities. She would face the pain, the fear and the disappointment head-on. Because only then would she recognize the wonderful moments to come.

"Oh, my!" Fran exclaimed, tearing Cathy from her reverie.

Cathy's pulse revved to life as she watched her friend's hand fly to her belly. "What's wrong?"

Fran's eyes were as bright as diamonds. "The baby kicked."

A soft gasp escaped Cathy's throat. "May I feel?"

"Of course."

Gingerly, she placed her palm on Fran's protruding tummy. In seconds, she felt a knock against her hand, felt the life growing inside her new sister. For a moment, Cathy closed her eyes. But when she saw a child with milk-chocolate eyes and a devilish grin in her mind, she opened them and stepped away.

With an aching heart, she asked Fran, "Do you know if you're having a boy or a girl?"

"I am having a Nicholas Steven Maxim Thorne."

Cathy clasped her hands together. "Oh, Fran. A boy!"

Beaming, Fran exclaimed, "I know. I can't wait."

"Aunt Cathy. I really like that."

"And I really like having a sister."

Cathy gave her a gentle hug. "Me, too. I always wanted a sister. Long talks about boys, shared confidences about taffy addictions."

On a round of giggles, they both turned back to

Gershin's window, watched a batch of caramel taffy being pulled.

Fran put a hand to the glass. "Did Max ever tell you about the time I went in there and pulled the taffy?"

"Only like a hundred times. He loves your free spirit and your dedication."

"And to think, I love him for his fine, fine backside and the way he makes my knees go weak when he kisses me."

Cathy glanced over, smiled.

"That smile didn't reach your eyes, little sister."

"No?"

Fran shook her head. "You really miss him, huh?"

Cathy lifted her chin. "Miss who?"

Fran grinned. "Coy doesn't work on you, Cathy. The deputy marshal, the one that rescued you, protected you from Cale and Peter."

Cathy's heart dipped. Did she miss him? Did a fish miss the water when it was flopping about on land? "He doesn't want to have anything to do with me."

"And what do you want?"

"Oh, Fran, I want a life of my own choosing. But most of all, I want a life with him."

"Have you told your father that?"

Cathy recalled the two-hour discussion she'd had with her father after the royal physician had thoroughly checked her out. "I've told him that I'm in charge of my life and my *love* life now, and that I intend to set my own schedule."

Admiration filled Fran's eyes. "How did he take it?"

"He was surprised at my firm stance. But I know I gained his respect." She smiled. "But most important, I gained my own."

"Did you tell him about your feelings for the marshal?"

"No."

Fran didn't press her further. Thankfully, she spotted the other half of their trek-into-town group, and was pulling Cathy over to them.

"The two most beautiful ladies in the world." Cathy's brother Max gave his wife a kiss before glancing over at the bodyguards, hovering a few yards away.

"I am famished," Aunt Fara announced, rubbing at a bit of sunburn on her regal left shoulder. "Where shall we go?"

"How about the Belltower?" Max suggested.

Fran shook her head. "Your son wants clam chowder."

Ranen, Cathy's crusty old godfather, nodded his approval. "Sounds good to me."

Max shrugged. "Clam chowder it is, then."

As Max and Fran shared a few newlywed kisses, Cathy sidled up beside Ranen and gave him a kiss on his weathered cheek.

The old curmudgeon frowned, not an unusual occurrence. "Well, running off to the mountains of Colorado. That was a fine spectacle you made of yourself, young lady."

Cathy smiled. "I did my best."

Fara put a hand on her niece's shoulder. "Don't pay him any mind, Catherine."

"Oh, I never do, Auntie."

A mask of surprise lit Ranen's features. "Look at this. The young lady has a defiant tongue on her."

"It's about time, don't you think?" Cathy said boldly.

Everyone stopped talking, their attention now focused on Cathy and Ranen.

"Perhaps." A sweep of admiration passed over Ranen's eyes.

Fara wrapped an arm around Cathy, pulled her close and said for all to hear, "Your young man has brought out a new side in you, my dear. I quite like it."

Cathy sighed, laughed in spite of herself. "Does everyone know about…well, my young man?"

Fara smiled gracefully.

Ranen rolled his eyes.

"Not Alex," Max offered. "But he's in Scotland."

Fran laughed.

Cathy groaned.

Max chuckled. "Come on. Let's go eat. The longer we stand here, the more chance my wife has to contemplate feeding our child taffy for lunch."

Cathy watched Fran punch her husband lightly in the arm, her eyes overflowing with love. She watched as Max bent and kissed Fran again, then mouthed the words, "I love you."

And as they walked along toward the beach restaurant, Cathy watched her grumpy godfather take Fara's hand in his.

Cathy smiled at the couples, but her heart felt heavy, for it desperately missed its other half.

* * *

"Thank you for seeing me, Your Royal Highness."

"It's my pleasure, Deputy Mason."

"Dan, please."

Seated in a weathered leather chair in the palace library, the king nodded. "You saved my daughter's life, Dan. I owe you much. Have you come to collect the reward?"

"Reward?" Dan asked.

"One million American dollars." The king chuckled. "You act as though you've never heard of this."

"I haven't." As though he'd accept anything for caring and protecting Angel. She'd given him everything he could ask for—in her smile, her kindness, her devotion to all things good and right. "No, thanks, Your Highness."

"You're looking for more?" the king asked coldly.

"No. I want nothing, sir." Dan sighed, raked a hand through his hair. "Well, that's not exactly true."

"Speak plainly."

"I want a job."

Royal eyebrows shot upward. "A job?"

"That's right."

The formidable man studied him for a moment, then said, "You wish to be close to Catherine."

Dan hesitated.

"There's no reason to deny it, young man. I know about you. I have heard about you…about your past."

Dan's jaw went tight as a trap, but he fought through it. "All right. I want to be close to her, sir." He leaned forward in his chair and got real with the king of Llandaron. "I love your daughter like I've never loved anything or anyone. I want to marry her, have children with her, grow old, sit in a rocker out on the palace porch.''

A smile tugged at the king's mouth, but he shuttered the look immediately.

''Now, I know that I'm nowhere good enough for her,'' Dan continued. ''But I don't care about that anymore. Fact is, she loves me and I love her. Fact is, I can make her happy. That's got to count for something.''

The king rubbed his beard thoughtfully. ''It counts for much.''

''But I'm not going into this. I'm not going to ask her to be my wife unless I have something, unless I have a—''

''A job?'' the king provided.

Dan nodded. ''Yes, sir.''

The king sighed. ''I admire a man who's willing to give up his life, his past for my daughter.''

''I appreciate that, sir. And if you're willing to listen, I've got an idea.''

The king sat back in his chair, righted his glasses. ''Well, I think I would very much like to hear it.''

With her hair falling in loose curls around her shoulders, Cathy slipped into a beautiful gown of lavender silk. She didn't feel much like a party, but with the governor of California in town, her father had made a grand gesture. And besides, she wanted to talk to the governor about a program she was developing for low-income housing in Los Angeles.

A program that would change much and demand many months of her time. A welcome directive, as it would keep her mind occupied and her heart shuttered.

A knock at the door snatched her from her thoughts.

"Just a moment, Cale," she called, fastening an earring as she made her way to the door.

But when she opened it, it wasn't her bodyguard who stood before her in a tailored black tuxedo.

"Dan?" The word, that wonderful word, came out in a breathless gasp. Was she hallucinating? Had she dreamed of seeing him so many times that now her mind had concocted his image?

He gave a little bow. "Good evening, Your Highness."

The only way she could think of to see if he was really there was to touch him. Her heart in her throat, she reached out, sighed when she felt his skin, his cheek.

"Angel." On a groan, he dragged her into his arms, kissed her hungrily, turned her knees to butter.

For a moment, one glorious moment, she let herself fall under his spell, let her mouth be taken and nibbled and branded. She was back in the mountains, in his bed, beneath him. But in the back of her mind, a voice urged her to return to the present.

With her hands to his chest, she eased herself back slightly. "What are you doing here?"

He smiled. "I've come to escort you to the ballroom."

"Not here at my door, but here in Llandaron."

"New job."

"Dan Mason!"

He pulled her close again. "All right, Angel."

She melted against him, felt his heart beat.

He kissed her forehead softly, where the bruise of her past had almost faded. "I lied to you, too. I am tired of running. I am tired of living in the past. I want a future."

His words warmed her soul, spreading heat to every muscle, every bone, making all those deeply hidden wishes and wants she'd had since she'd met him flutter to the surface.

"I quit the marshal service, I quit Denver and I refuse to have a life without you."

Without her? Her pulse quickened. She glanced up. "What are you saying?"

"I'm the new head of palace security." He touched her face, brushed his thumb across her mouth, which had dropped open at his announcement. "Your bodyguard, Angel. And I'd like to be your husband, if you'll let me be."

Tears sprang to her eyes. Not from pain or loneliness or frustration, but from happiness. "I love you so much."

"And I love you," he said tenderly. "Can you forgive me for acting like such a stupid, scared jackass?"

She nodded. "If you can forgive me for being a stupid, scared jackass."

On a chuckle, he pulled her closer. "Done."

She reached up on her tippy toes, kissed him, then sighed. "I can't believe you're really here."

"Well, I am. In fact, I'm having Rancon brought over, and a year's supply of Chef Boyardee."

She laughed. "S'mores, too?"

"Of course." He kissed her mouth softly. "My life is here with you now. So you see, you're going to have to marry me, Angel."

The tears brimming in her eyes slipped down her cheeks. "Yes."

"How about tonight? Or right now, that is, if your father would allow it?"

Her chin lifted. "No one decides my future for me anymore, Dan. I make my own choices now."

He grinned, eased away from her and slipped a hand in his pocket. Moments later, he held out the most perfect, most beautiful amethyst ring Cathy had ever seen.

"It's so beautiful," she said breathlessly, her heart swelling with love as she watched him slip the ring on her finger.

For a brief second she thought of the old woman and her predictions, of all the things that had been lost in this journey and of the two people that had truly been found. But then Dan gathered her into his arms, kissed her deeply and made her forget all.

When they finally came up for air, he whispered, "Should we go and tell your family?"

With a winsome smile, Cathy pulled him farther inside her bedroom, then closed the door behind him. "I don't think I'm ready to share you yet."

"No?"

"No," she said on a breathless laugh.

He grinned like the devil. "Did I tell you I want a ton of kids?"

"All of them with your chin."

"Your eyes."

"Your mouth."

"Your hair."

With a quick smile, she turned, gave him her back. "Shall we get started right now?"

"Is that a command, Your Highness?"

"Just an offer, my love."

"Well, that's an offer I could never refuse!" On a growl, Dan slowly unzipped her dress, searing kisses down her neck and back as he went. And when they were both naked and wrapped in each other's arms in her bed, Cathy felt at peace for the first time in her life. At peace, on fire, in love and looking into a future of her own choosing with the man of her dreams beside her.

And who knew? she mused, gasping with pleasure as Dan slid inside her. Perhaps they were creating that future, creating their first child, right now...

*   *   *   *   *

And now,
Turn the page for a preview
Of Laura Wright's
Next sensual Fiery Tale

RULING PASSIONS

Available in September 2003
From Silhouette Desire

Prologue

The sea took the shape of a woman's hip as it climbed into a wave: curved and pink from the coming sunset. But Crown Prince Alexander William Charles Octavos Thorne had no use for women anymore, real or imagined.

Lungs filled with salty air, he sagged against a jagged rock and watched the surf crash against the beach and crawl toward him.

He didn't run from its progress, didn't move. Not even when icy water stung his foot.

He understood the sea's endless need to consume, to take, to hurt. For five long years, he'd felt the like—too many times to count. Then there was today…

Three hours ago, he'd received word that his wife had left town, left him for another man. Like the cold, pinkish waves before him, relief rippled through his blood. Relief and anger—for a woman who'd hated him the minute they'd married, a woman who'd acted like a bloody iceberg no matter how hard he'd try to care for her—for a woman who'd wanted no children, no warmth, no friendship.

Alex tore off his shirt, let the cool air rush over his chest.

He'd been a man of his word, married a woman he'd hardly known, remained loyal and honorable to her, kept silent when she'd told his father and the court that they were trying to conceive a child—even kept up the charade that they'd been living together for the last two years.

But today, on the day she'd run off with another man, loyalty, honor and care went to Llandaron only. Alex had his country to think of now, damage control to see to. If the world found out the truth of his situation, the heart of the Llandaron people could be destroyed forever.

Pretense was his only saving grace.

He would move slowly, tread easily. He would use whatever money and means was required to settle this matter, while keeping the truth hidden for as long as possible. Next week he left for his summit with the Emperor of Japan. He would make his wife's excuses, take care of business, and while he was there, call in a favor from an old school chum he trusted who just happened to be a divorce barrister in London. Then at some point, he'd return home to Llandaron and tell his family—tell his father that he'd failed.

At that offensive realization, Alex's jaw tightened

to the point of pain. If there was anything he despised more than failure it was admitting that he had.

Echoing his mood, twilight seeped in around him and the sea turned choppy, each boundless curl morphing from pale pink to violent purple.

From this day forward, he vowed silently, no woman would rule him.

From this day forward, he would rule nothing.

The life-long yearning to govern his country would now be put aside in favor of his brother, Maxim. For a Queen and an heir were vital to the Kingdom of Llandaron. And Maxim had both.

Pain snapped at Alex's heart. He opened his mouth and released five years of unlivable ache. The gut-wrenching cries to the sea echoed, ricocheting back into his ears, making him start, stop.

Suddenly, his eyes widened, focused. All thought drifted down, sank into the wet sand under his feet as out in the distance, twenty feet or so, a sailboat lurched across the coarse sea.

For one brief moment, before the boat disappeared behind the towering cove walls, he saw a woman, perched on the bow of the craft like one of the jewel-tailed mermaids from his childhood dreams, all mind-blowing curves and long, red hair.

She was facing him, hair thrashing about her neck and chest like silken whips. She seemed to stare straight at him—a bizarre sensation, as her eyes were impossible to make out. Unlike the detectable combination of senses emanating from her; air, water and fire.

From gut to groin Alex went hard.

A massive wave crashed just inches from him, spitting saltwater into his face, his mouth and eyes. He scrubbed a hand over his face to clear the mist, then quickly glanced up.

Both boat and mermaid were gone.

Awareness, raw and demanding, battled in his blood, but he shoved the feeling away. He'd felt need before, perhaps not this strong, but he'd fight it just the same. No woman would rule him.

Jaw set, Alex stripped bare and dove into the frigid water, determined to remind the lower half of him—just as he had his mind—who was master.

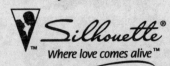

ERICA SPINDLER

D E A D R U N

USA TODAY *bestselling author Erica Spindler proves
once again that she is a master at delivering
chilling shockers that explore the sometimes
twisted nature of the human psyche.*

When Rachel Ames disappears after leaving a strange message on
her sister's answering machine, Liz Ames heads to Key West to find
out what's happened. Within days of her arrival, the area is plagued
by a mysterious suicide, another disappearance and the brutal murder
of a teenage girl. But no one believes these events are linked to
Rachel's disappearance.

Only Rick Wells, a former cop, is willling to listen to Liz. And as they
get closer to the truth, they begin to uncover an unspeakable evil from
which they may not escape unscathed.

"…savvy amounts of sex and moral outrage, investigagtion and con-
frontation, psychology and romance." —*Publishers Weekly*

On sale in May 2003 wherever paperbacks are sold!

MIRA®

MES683

COMING NEXT MONTH